REMEMBRANCES OF WARS PAST
A War Veterans Anthology

REMEMBRANCES OF WARS PAST
A WAR VETERANS ANTHOLOGY

edited by

Henry F. Tonn

Fox Track Publications
Wilmington, North Carolina

Fox Track Publications
c/o Henry F. Tonn
4608 Cedar Ave., Suite 110
Wilmington, NC 28403

First Edition

Cover design by Kevin Morgan Watson

Cover art, "Soldier Overlooks the Horizon," by Chris Downie,
ninjaMonkeyStudio, licensed for use through iStock.
All rights reserved.

Printed on acid-free paper

ISBN 978-1-935708-70-4 (paperback)
ISBN 978-1-935708-71-1 (hardcover)

In memory of my mother,
May Tonn,
who married the wrong man
and paid the highest price
for her mistake.

ACKNOWLEDGMENTS

The following works in this anthology have been previously published.

"Abu Ghraib Suggests the Isenheim Altarpiece," *Southern California Review*

"Beirut Pastoral," *Approximately Paradise*

"Benzedrine," *Iconoclast* and *The Santa Cruz Sentinel*

"Buchenwald Diary," *Connecticut Review*

"Dear Mr. Sandman," *Connecticut Review* and *Red Fields* MEP 2012

"Faith," *34th Parallel*

"Friday Night FOB Cobra," *Willow Springs Review*

"Gun Point," *Red Fields* MEP 2012

"I Heard a Fly Buzz," *Red Fields* MEP 2012

"Japanese October," *Oasis*

"Observation Post," *Willow Springs Review*

"One Bullet," *label me latin*

"Parkie, Tanker, Tiger of Tobruk," *A Collection of Friends*

"Sarajevo Roses," *Writer's Digest* and *2010 Press 53 Open Awards Anthology*

"Small Fires – Nagasaki," *Zorba's Daughter*

"Spring in Jalula," *The Kenyon Review*

"That Saigon Night," *The Deadly Writer's Patrol*

"The Hungry Ghosts," *Amazon Shorts*

"The Last Civilized Battle," *American Society of the French Legion of Honor* newsletter

"The Two Things I Wanted," *NAM: Things That Weren't True and Other Stories*

"Veterans," *The Kerf. California: College of the Redwoods*

"What's for Dinner, Doc?" *Red Fields* MEP 2012

REMEMBRANCES OF WARS PAST
A WAR VETERANS ANTHOLOGY

POETRY

Introduction

The genesis of this anthology goes back to 2009 when I was watching a football game in the man-cave of my eighty-eight-year-old friend, Richard Daughtry. During commercials Dick would regale me with tales of his World War II experiences, particularly his tour of the Buchenwald concentration camp one day after it was liberated in 1945. It seemed to me that some of these memories should be written up for posterity, so one evening Dick and I got it all down on tape. Shortly thereafter, I committed the story to paper.

In the fall of 2010 the *Connecticut Review* came out with a special section of prose and poetry written by veterans of war. They accepted Daughtry's story and I eventually received my complimentary copy. The quality of work literally stunned me. People risking their lives to defend our country could write like this? I suggested to the editor that a book anthology of this nature should be produced, and she agreed but found little interest from publishers. Publishing companies did not want to take a chance on this kind of project given the prevailing uncertainties in the industry. So I decided to produce the anthology myself because I believe it *ought* to be done.

In February of 2012 I created a website and advertised my proposed anthology in a variety of online publications. Over the next three months I received 500 submissions of fiction, nonfiction, and poetry from 150 writers. During the first two weeks, the submissions arrived at such a prodigious rate I had a full-blown panic attack. I wondered if I had dived into waters entirely too deep for my abilities.

Everything eventually stabilized, however, and in the end I accepted twenty-two pieces of prose and twenty-three of poetry, covering a wide variety of wars, with the Vietnam and Iraq wars being most represented. There was a bias toward well-written pieces dealing with some aspect of armed conflict heretofore underreported. I chose interesting stories and moving poetry with visceral content rather than more passive or emotionally detached works. But several pieces were included for their originality and fresh use of language. The result is a cross section of material that enriches the reader from a literary standpoint while simultaneously offering an educational experience.

The best of all worlds.

—Henry F. Tonn

REMEMBRANCES OF WARS PAST
A War Veterans Anthology

Bass Fishing on the Mekong
~ Russell Reece ~

The sun hovered over the sweltering Mekong Delta as our landing craft snaked up a jungle-lined tributary. Under the drone of the diesel engine we searched the edge of the tangled shoreline.

A pilot had reported seeing two bodies in this area. Wardel, Jenkins, and I were with the Army Graves Registration unit out of Qui-Nhon and had been sent in to recover them. The gunners-mate, the boat coxswain, and the ensign were Navy, attached to the landing craft USS Sussex County, on station nearby in the Mekong River.

There had been heavy fighting in this region over the last couple of months and it was now designated as cleared of enemy fighters. But as the stream narrowed and the jungle loomed over the water, you had to wonder just how they knew that. Everyone in the boat was on high alert. We came around a bend and the coxswain pointed, "There they are."

Two bloated bodies, Marines, lay together near the opening of a small ravine at the edge of the water. They were both in their camo pants and dark green tee shirts; one was face down in the mud, his legs still on the bank. The other man was on top of the first, crumpled into a semi-fetal position.

"Can you get the boat in there?" the ensign asked the coxswain. Trees and branches extended into the water.

"I can get close," he said. "But the boys are going to have to get their feet wet."

"Let's do it."

The machine-gunner stood ready on the thirty-caliber. We raised our weapons as the boat headed toward shore. Ten feet away, the coxswain jammed the motor in reverse and revved the engine. The boat drifted into the shallows and stopped in a tangle of submerged limbs and branches, twenty-five feet from the ravine. The engine continued to thrum and sputter in the water as the coxswain lowered the bow-ramp. The stench of rotting flesh wafted into the open boat.

"Okay, Perez. Let's make this quick," the ensign said. "Supposed to be cleared out around here but I wouldn't bet on it."

"Yes, sir," I said.

"Oh, shit," the coxswain said as the smell reached him. "God, that's bad." He wrapped his fingers around his nose and mouth.

"Get on with it!" the ensign said. He moved to the back of the boat.

I stayed on the ramp and unfolded the heavy body-bag as Wardel and Jenkins made their way through the ankle-deep water, ducking and twisting around the thick jungle brush. In the ravine, Jenkins held back as Wardel squatted down and inspected the bodies. He slipped his hand between the two dead men, felt around, then moved to the other side and did it again.

"What's he doing?" the ensign said. This was his first experience with combat remains.

"Checking for booby traps," I said.

Wardel stood up and motioned to Jenkins who joined him. They turned the top man over and Jenkins grabbed him by the arm and slid him off into the mud. Jenkins retreated again as Wardel carefully rolled the second man onto his side. "We're clear," he said. Jenkins rejoined Wardel and they both grabbed the man under his armpits and pulled him toward the boat, his boots dragging, his stiff, outstretched arm catching awkwardly against saplings and branches. Five feet away, Jenkins slipped and fell face down into the water. "Goddamn it!" he said as he pushed himself back up. He pulled a handful of sea-weedy muck from the neck of his flack-jacket. "Son of a bitch!"

Wardel laughed. "Quit fooling around, Jenkins. We've got work to do here."

"Fuck you, Wardel!"

Wardel chuckled as they brought the man the rest of the way and the three of us lifted him onto the open body bag. I did a quick ID check, found his dog-tags and made a note. Then we straightened things up as much as we could. Cartilage crunched as Jenkins forced the man's arm against his chest. Behind me, one of the guys in the boat crew muttered. I zippered the bag shut.

"These boys been shot in the head," Wardel said. "Prisoners, I'll bet."

"That's how they ended up piled together," I said.

The three of us lifted the heavy load by the sewn-in handles and laid it on the deck against the bulkhead. I unfolded another bag as Wardel and Jenkins went back for the second man. When they got to him Jenkins reached down but Wardel stiffened and held up his hand. He was focused on a spot farther up the ravine.

"Look alive!" The ensign said. I turned to see him shoulder his M14. The gunners-mate swung the machine gun toward the ravine. I grabbed my weapon and looked back. Jenkins had squatted down and pulled out his pistol. Wardel was hunched over, gun in hand, picking his way slowly along the bank. Then he stopped, straightened up and waved us off. He holstered his piece. We all breathed a sigh of relief.

They brought the dead man back, and as Jenkins and I were getting him organized onto the bag, Wardel sat on the ramp and scanned the edge of the river. "You ever go bass fishing, Perez?" he asked.

"Yeah. My grandfather lived on a lake in Michigan."

"That's cool. Down in Arkansas I fish the lower Spring River. It looks a lot like this." He pointed at the broken shoreline, the windblown trees extending into the water. "Those'd be hot spots right there, lots of structure; good places for bass to hide. I'd get in there with my johnboat, work all the possibilities."

"Jigging and Pigging, eh?" Jenkins said.

Wardel grinned and gave Jenkins a friendly shove. "You know about it, don't you?"

"Move the leg so I can get this zippered," I said to Jenkins.

He rolled the man on his side and the edges of the bag came together.

"There's two things I take seriously, Wardel," Jenkins said. "Fishing and fucking."

"Shit. You might know about fishing, but no woman's gonna go anywhere near your stinky ass. Here, watch this." Wardel pantomimed holding a rod and making a cast. He waited for the bait to hit the water. "Ploop," he said. He cranked his imaginary reel and then set the hook on a fish. "Look at that, first cast." He slapped Jenkins on the chest and chuckled.

"Let's wrap this up," the ensign said. He stood next to us, a rag over his nose and mouth, his gaze deliberately avoiding the dead man.

Wardel looked up at him. "There's another one, sir."

"What?"

Wardel nodded toward the ravine. "It's just around the corner, lying in the water."

"Well, goddamn it, go get it and let's get the hell out of here." The ensign went back to the stern and, facing the river, removed the rag for a few seconds and took a deep breath.

I ID'd the second guy and cleaned off some of the river muck that had accumulated on the body. I zippered the bag and the three of us laid it on the deck next to the first.

Wardel nodded at me. "The next one's been there a while. Must have been a floater. Ain't going to be as pretty as the last two."

"You need me to come with you," I said.

"There's nowhere for you to work. We'll bring the guy out."

It took a little while for them to reach the third body. They broke branches and tossed debris out of the way to clear a path. Then they were behind the bank and all we could see were their heads and shoulders.

"When's this fucking nightmare going to be over?" the gunner said to no one in particular.

I turned around. He was in the gun turret, looking down on us. He wiped his forehead and flicked grimy sweat from his fingers.

"How did we end up with this funeral gig, anyway?" he said.

"Stow it, Rico," the ensign said. He put the rag back over his nose.

The coxswain stared back at me, expressionless. The engine continued to burble and sputter at the stern.

I looked toward the ravine. Wardel and Jenkins were heading to the boat, carrying the corpse by its belt and the neck of its flack-jacket. The head dangled down and wobbled when they walked as if it were connected by a thin strand. Both arms were gone, one from the shoulder, one just above the elbow. Foul bugs and entrails dropped and splattered into the shallow water. An eye was missing and some of the facial flesh had been cleaned to the bone.

"Jesus Christ," the gunner said.

Wardel and Jenkins carefully placed the body on the open bag and organized things. The guy had been blown up. I tried to find some ID but there was nothing obvious. We'd have to look more closely when we got him back to the unit.

Jenkins got the bag closed around the legs and started the zipper. I finished it off and we laid the bag next to the other two. I gave the ensign the thumbs up. He started to say something but then leaned over the side, retched several times, and vomited into the river.

Wardel, Jenkins and I sat down on the deck against the side bulkhead. Jenkins shook a cigarette from his pack and offered it to Wardel. The coxswain lifted the ramp, revved the engine hard in reverse, and the boat slowly pulled away from shore.

The ensign wiped his face and sat down next to us on a rusted toolbox. He removed his helmet and stared at the bags. He was shaking. "Sorry," he said.

The gunner put the safety on the thirty. He lit a cigarette and took a long drag as we headed back to the ship.

BUCHENWALD DIARY
~ Henry F. Tonn ~
from the verbal history of Richard Daughtry

In April, 1945, while General George Patton and the U.S. Army were racing across Europe in pursuit of the German infantry, I was a technical sergeant in the 377 fighter squadron, a part of Patton's left flank support. The support missions had been slowing down of late, and we were finding ourselves with progressively more leisure time. One day a group of us was gathered by the side of the road next to the airfield shooting the bull and watching the traffic pass by. Suddenly, a jeep screeched to a halt in front of us and the driver blurted out, "They are burning up people back there." We asked him several questions and he mentioned a prison camp near the town of Weimar, then drove off excitedly.

We thought this was peculiar and wanted to find out more, so the five of us went to the executive officer and asked him if we could check out the story. Frankly, we had nothing better to do. He seemed interested himself and said he would authorize a two-and-a-half-ton truck to make the trip if we could find ten more soldiers interested in the mission. It didn't take us long to round up the necessary people, and so all the arrangements were made.

The next morning we got up early and started on our way. We brought enough "C" rations to last us for twenty-four hours, plus several cartons of cigarettes each. Not all of us smoked, but cigarettes—along with chocolate bars—were the major form of barter during the Second World War. The trip took about three hours and was relatively uneventful, except that we noticed there were no American troops around. This made us a bit apprehensive, a feeling that grew when we reached the outskirts of Weimar and spied two American soldiers lying in a ditch pinned down by sniper fire. Apparently, the area was not exactly secured, and isolated skirmishes were still occurring.

We decided not to stop or turn around, and instead plowed ahead toward Weimar until we reached the city limits, then we drove east for about five miles until we arrived at the main gate of the concentration camp known as Buchenwald. Two American solders greeted us. After checking our credentials, they informed us that only a few military personnel had been left behind to guard the area. More would be arriving shortly, however. They suggested if we had only the afternoon for observation, we ought to begin with the crematorium because it was one of the closest buildings, and we could visit some of the barracks from there.

It wasn't hard to locate the crematorium since it had a huge chimney stretching skyward and a high wooden fence surrounding it. It was a cold, overcast day and we were all wearing heavy overcoats. We noted prisoners wandering aimlessly about the compound, mostly emaciated, wearing tattered clothing, their faces essentially blank. They had been liberated only the day before and really didn't know what to do with themselves. Suddenly three prisoners walked up and began speaking to us in excellent English. Two were Jewish and wearing striped prison garb with a yellow star of David over their hearts. The other was from Poland and had a dilapidated tan uniform. They looked remarkably healthy and strong given the pathetic state that most of their fellow inmates were in. I later learned that they were the educated members of the camp and had been used by the Nazis to perform office work; consequently, they were well fed and taken care of. After speaking to us briefly, the two Jewish men insisted on being our guides, saying they wanted to make certain the atrocities that had occurred in this camp were viewed and recorded for history by all who visited the place.

Bypassing the crematorium momentarily, they steered us first to a nearby building. We immediately found ourselves in a room something like twenty by forty feet, with a large number of prisoners seated on the floor, backs to the wall, shoulder to shoulder, staring vacantly into space. They were all wearing nightshirts that fell just below their knees.

They were incredibly thin, seeming to be no more than four feet tall, weighing no more than sixty pounds, and their eyes were sunk deeply into the sockets of their heads. We were absolutely stunned. We asked our guides what had happened and they responded that all of these men had been starved into this condition. At the camp you either worked or were shot, so the men had worked to the point of death.

We offered to give them food but the guides shook their heads and said their bodies could no longer accept nourishment. Upon liberation of the camp the previous day, several of them had been fed and they had died instantly. The guides estimated that most of the men in the room would expire in several more days. We asked if we could give them cigarettes and they shrugged and replied that it was unlikely they had enough strength to inhale the smoke. They were barely able to get enough oxygen in their bodies to survive. Nonetheless, we approached several of these people, whose eyes followed us in their dark sockets, and placed cigarettes in the mouths of those who appeared to be interested. As our guides had predicted, however, they were unable to puff, and the cigarettes just dangled there unsmoked.

I remember all this as being surreal. We were in that room for a half-hour or so but did very little talking. The guides spoke to us softly, telling about the atrocities that had been occurring in this camp for many years. I remember being numb; I couldn't absorb fully what was being said to me. It was just too bizarre. I wondered how human beings could treat each other like this. Every time we asked if there was anything we could do, the guides simply shook their heads and insisted we only needed to witness and remember.

Finally, we left and walked over to the crematorium which was located a short distance away. On entering the building we saw two brick structures, each containing three ovens. The ovens still harbored the remains of human beings that had been incinerated only recently. Body parts could be seen: some ribs still intact, portions of a skull. Apparently the people assigned to burn them had left in a hurry and the job had not been completed properly. On the opposite side of the room was a long wooden table covered with lampshades of tattooed skin. There were five or ten of them—I can't remember exactly—all in a row. The skin had been stretched around the lampshades and attached in some way. One of the guides explained that this was the work of Ilse Koch, the ex-commandant's wife, later known as the Beast of Buchenwald. She had men with elaborate tattoos on their chests killed, the skin stripped off, dried, and then made into lampshades. One of the guides even pointed out a nipple on one of the shades. It was eerie. We spent most of our time in the crematorium at that table. I remember handling several of the lampshades. I also remember a shrunken head on the table. I later learned that shrunken heads were usually fashioned from murdered Russian POWs.

In recent years I've seen a picture of a table with various assorted items on it, and one lampshade. I read that at the trial of Ilse Koch they could not produce any of those lampshades and thus that particular charge against her was dismissed for lack of evidence. What happened to the lampshades? Did somebody take them as souvenirs? They were certainly there on the day I toured the facility.

After touring the crematorium, we walked out a side door and to our left and found a stack of bodies apparently waiting to be cremated. They were thrown together in a pell-mell fashion, a pile of them about four or five feet high, all emaciated. Some looked as if they had been recently killed—they were bloody and such, but others looked like older corpses. Interestingly enough, on top of the pile were two German guards fully clothed. All insignia had been ripped from their uniforms, and I assumed they were taken as souvenirs, though I don't know that for sure. It is a fact that American soldiers were known to take souvenirs during this war. In any event, we were told by our guides that these two guards had been captured by the American army the day before on the road to Weimar and were brought back to the camp. They were then put in a room with ten prisoners armed with billy clubs, whereupon the prisoners beat them to death. I could tell they had been beaten because their faces were all puffy and bloody. In subsequent pictures, I never saw those German guards on that stack of bodies. I assume they were removed because it would have reflected poorly on the American army. But they were there on April twelfth when I toured the facility, and that part of history has never been told, to my knowledge.

A short distance away we came upon a flatbed trailer piled high with dead bodies. These bodies were stacked very neatly in a row, head to foot, foot to head, alternately. I wondered if they were the next pile of bodies to be delivered to the crematorium as soon as the other pile had been burned. We didn't stay there very long because how many emaciated bodies can you look at? We asked our guides if they could take us into some of the nearby barracks, and then we broke up into different groups with different guides.

The first one we visited had a half-dozen or so prisoners in the bunks, not very many, and they weren't moving. I never knew if they were sleeping or dead, and I never asked. We then passed on to a number of other barracks rapidly because we wanted to see all we could in the limited time we had left, and found most of them to be pretty much the same. Each had a few prisoners but none were moving. The guide warned us eventually not to proceed any further than barracks forty-five or so because the Germans had been conducting medical experiments there, injecting the prisoners with typhus, and an epidemic had broken out. It was still possible to catch the fever if you ventured there.

We left and walked across the yard. Prisoners milled about, their faces displaying no expression, showing no interest in us whatsoever. Most were gaunt, but a few looked relatively healthy. I've seen movies where the prisoners showed great jubilation upon liberation, but there was none of that on this day. I asked one of the guards why they were so quiet and relatively grim given that they had been liberated. He replied that the jubilation had occurred on the previous day when the liberation had actually occurred, and now they were confronted with their futures. "They have nowhere to go," he said.

I gave the Jewish prisoner who had been my primary guide a carton of cigarettes and you would have thought he had died and gone to heaven—though that's probably a poor choice of words in this particular context. But he was very happy. I noted that there was no bad odor permeating the place throughout our afternoon there. I read later that people reported Buchenwald had this horrible stench that hung over it when it was liberated and later on when people visited the camp. Well, maybe so, but there was no stench the day we made our tour. I don't know if it was because the furnaces weren't burning or because the temperature that day hovered around thirty degrees and everything was frozen, or some combination of the two, but I distinctly remember there being no noxious odor.

It was beginning to get dark so we piled back into the truck and drove into Weimar to find a place to sleep for the night. A goodly number of troops from the Third Army were there now, even though earlier when we had passed through the town we had seen only those two soldiers in the ditch. We came upon a group of Americans who were warming themselves by a fire, so we stopped and warmed our "C" rations and asked them about a place to stay. They pointed to several abandoned buildings on the same block and said we should occupy one of them. So, after we ate, we found a building to our liking and settled in around six o'clock in the evening. The room we were in had no furniture and we slept on the hard floor, but that didn't bother any of us because we were used to sleeping on hard floors. You just wrapped yourself in your overcoat, turned on your side, and went to sleep. Unfortunately, a fire fight broke out in the street about midnight and I didn't get much sleep after that. I was in the Air Force and was used to being bombed and strafed, but I was not used to being shot at with small armed weapons. It scared me to death, and I was particularly fearful of somebody lobbing a grenade into our room and blowing us all up. I ended up huddled against the wall in a far corner of that room, shivering with fear, and wishing to hell that I'd never come to this town. I was afraid the Germans would re-take the place and capture all of us, and we would end up in a prison camp ourselves. What a hell of an irony that would have been!

By the morning, though, everything had cleared up and scads of Third Army personnel were combing the streets. We decided to walk around and see the city. At noontime we noticed a number of trucks had been brought up and the civilians of Weimar were being escorted into the trucks to be taken out to Buchenwald to witness the atrocities. The civilians weren't happy about it but they were often being escorted at gunpoint. I read later that General Patton came through several days later and threw such a fit at what he saw that he ordered all the civilians of that city to walk the five miles to the camp to see what had been going on. Maybe so, but some of them had already made the trip because I saw them board the trucks.

We enjoyed the sites of Weimar all day—it was a beautiful city even though some buildings had been destroyed here and there, and we didn't leave until darkness was already falling. Looking back on it, the thing that affected me the most on that April twelfth was seeing that room full of people who were still alive but beyond hope. I had seen plenty of dead bodies during the war, so piles of emaciated bodies prepared for incineration did not affect me particularly. But looking into the sunken eyes of a man who has no hope of living because of circumstances beyond his control, that affected me in the most profound way.

It's an experience I'll never forget, and it changed me forever.

ABU GHRAIB SUGGESTS THE ISENHEIM ALTARPIECE
Elisabeth Murawski

Arms behind him shackled to the wall,
Jamadi's knees buckle. He lands on air.
Let us reposition him to stand erectly,

homo sapiens, place the irons higher up
on the window bars. When again he falls
forward, hangs like Jesus from his wrists,

call it faking, possum-playing. Persist.
Lift him up on legs that ragdoll-sag
into a third collapse, the effect

grotesque as Grunewald's Christ: bones
about to pop from their sockets. The silence
curious, raise the hood that hid a face,

asphyxiation, wag a finger past the eyes.
It has begun, the turning of the skin
to purple, the indigo of Tyre and Sidon. Note

as he's lowered to the floor, the stunning
rush of blood from nose and mouth,
the Red Sea. In this heat, let us blur

the time of death, pack the flesh in ice
like fish or meat, pretend he's merely
sick, hooked to an I.V., a patient

on a stretcher. Destroy the crime scene.
Throw away the bloodied hood. It stings
with the quality of mercy.

Note: This poem is based on material in "A Deadly Interrogation," by Jane Mayer, The New
Yorker, *Nov. 14, 2005.*

SARAJEVO ROSES
~ Kirk Barrett ~

When a mortar explodes in the street, it leaves a unique pattern on the ground. The concrete scars look like pressed flowers. We call them Sarajevo Roses.

A fresh bouquet was left for us this morning. I stepped around it when I came back from the Holiday Inn—where we go to make a few phone calls, or to pick up and send faxes to our various friends. These days it's our only form of communication with anyone outside the city.

In the relative protection of our underground café, I share a letter sent to us from our friends on the enemy side, those who maintain B92, Radio Free Beograd. They write that the snipers in the hills surrounding our beautiful city of collapse and ruin get paid per target. Extra for children. One sniper interviewed by a French reporter—rebroadcast on B92—told of how he relished seeing the expression on a mother's face when her daughter, standing next to her, was shot.

It's important to be proud of one's work—to hold to one's convictions—even in the face of disputes to the contrary. And even in these troubling and difficult times, it is reassuring to know there is job security in Sarajevean Snipering. So many of us still remain here to become the intended targets in these circus games. We stay, continuing our daily rounds of Bosnian Roulette in our attempts to get water from the only remaining spigot in the city. Occasionally, due to the boredom of repetition, we set up other contests to pass the time competing with the snipers in the hills.

One street corner in particular is a favorite arcade for the sharp-shooters. Anyone crossing the river and coming into town on a trek for water—or trying to sneak out of the city before this tournament is over—has to pass through this crossroad. Quite a rewarding site for the proud snipers who are paid per head, extra for kids.

It was Plamen's idea really, though he'd never admit to it. That haggard old grump likes to claim that he doesn't care about anyone or anything anymore. Plamen is older than the rest of us, like a grandfather who's wise and sharp and funny. Used to always have dirt under his fingernails from digging in a flowerbed he tended on the roof of his apartment. Born in Beograd, he's lived in Sarajevo since he was four or five. He's over seventy now. A landscape of creased flesh and dark eyes, he smiles, yellowed teeth between the missing gaps. He's lost almost everything he's ever held dear: children, wife, friends, city. Yet he has never ceased counsel with the better angels of his nature.

He's been collecting linens for weeks now. To some it may look cold and peculiar for this old man to go sorting through the rubble of someone's bombed-out home and walk away with their bedsheets. But since, from most vantage points, Plamen *is* a crazy old man, no one says anything to the contrary. In an insane situation, it is perfectly natural to display behavior that would at other times be considered utterly deranged. Besides that, say those who knew him from that distant Utopian time of "Before the Siege," Plamen had been to the United States. As if that alone explained something fundamental about him.

Twenty-five and some years ago, Plamen went on holiday in the U.S. He travelled to that fabled land called California, returning with fantastic tales of music and girls and drugs. Certainly, he brought back evidence of the incredible music—miscellaneous LP records—and, to some, his behavior gave credence to his stories of rampant drug parties, but his exotic tales of seductive girls had to be taken completely on faith as no proof was evident. Plamen, you see, wanted to be a beatnik, and in Communist Jugoslavia, he was about as close as anyone had ever come to being a poetic bohemian.

He collected the bedsheets for a specific purpose, and encouraged others to do the same. "Bring them down to the café," he told everyone. Then, from the former candle shop next door, he scavenged an assortment of dyes. The buckets he needed for his surreptitious plan were plentiful; empty containers lay everywhere. The difficulty was finding those without bullet holes.

When he had enough bedsheets, Plamen asked as many people as possible to help. We were a little surprised at how many actually showed up at our little café, each hauling a hesitant smile and a headful of curiosity. In the darkness of this urban war-zone, that old self-proclaimed hippie graced everyone with a night of joyful diversion. Several dozen of us spent all night tie-dying bed-sheets.

In the last hours before dawn, we'd dyed twenty, thirty sheets in an incredible array of colors, and even though most of them were still wet, we tied them together to make two huge quilts. They looked like motley flags of some tattered nation.

Plamen pulled a few of us aside and told us that we had to take the tapestries to the top floor of the building on the corner of Kulovića street.

Climbing the stairs, we gasped for breath under the weight of so much damp linen, for none of us was as fit as we used to be back when we could eat every day. I almost wanted to curse Plamen asking us make this climb. But when we arrived at the top floor and looked out through the fragmented glass remaining in the window openings, we saw what he had intended all along.

Plamen had been there previously, and strung cable across from one building to the other. It turned out that in the bygone days long before the Siege he worked for the television station as an antenna installer. He still had tools and metal cables. Plamen rigged a pulley in one building and an anchor in the one across the street. A double-line of cable ran between them. Tying the bed-sheets to the coiled metal wire, we pulled them out the window until they all hung between the buildings, bright-colored sails thirty meters high, blinding the view from the hills of the pedestrian walkway below and reducing the sniper's profit margin to nothing.

The centerpiece of the quilt blinder was an old souvenir from Plamen's journey in the mythic '60s, to that fairy-tale land known as San Francisco. A red, white, and blue tapestry of a skull with a lightning bolt across its cranium; an emblem of the Grateful Dead. He told us the icon is called "Steal Your Face."

We laughed ourselves to tears.

I do not know if the dead in Sarajevo are grateful or not. But at least they no longer suffer through the funerary games of hunger and snipers and land-mines. As for the living—we walked across Kulovića street at a leisurely pace in the calming shadow and temporary protection of the bedsheet tapestry, feeling gratitude with every step.

Plamen, however, was no longer around to see it. He lingered too long on an early morning water run, losing that day's game of Bosnian Roulette. We joke that since he was an old man, the sniper didn't get paid very much.

Every spring, in years past, Plamen planted flowers in his tiny rooftop garden.

Roses were always his favorite.

I Heard a Fly Buzz

Jason Poudrier

I stare out
A sand-fogged windshield
The size of a postcard
At a scene that
Could be drawn
With one horizontal line.

A fly loops
Around the
Enclosed cab,
Buzzing; he lands
On my face.

Swat—miss.

He flies before
My eyes, mocking,
Moving freely
As I sit cramped.

He lands
On my ears,
Chin,
Lips.

I slowly open
My mouth.

His legs tickle
As he walks in.

—I close.

My first kill.

What's for Dinner, Doc?

Jason Poudrier

Inside my Coke-can-armored Humvee,
I swelter in my flack vest,
feeling like Bugs Bunny, boiling
in a bathtub-sized pot,
singing along with the dancing little Indian
who is preparing him for dinner.

The solemn Iraqi children
stare at me with
starving big, black eyes
with sleepless, deep, brown bags
on a dried-up palette,
which is accompanied
by their dance,
a synchronized, sombering
movement of the hand
tapping the tip of the tongue.

I tear off the corner
of a bag of Skittles from my MRE
and toss it so it spins
and sprinkles Skittles from the sky
like on the commercials
back home they know nothing about;
they scurry about
collecting the colorful candies,
then scamper off,
leaving subtle dimples
in the sand.

I ask my BC
where their parents are;
he tells me
they're awaiting us
behind the dunes,
and I wonder if
I made the right
turn in Albuquerque.

Parkie, Tanker, Tiger of Tobruk
~ Tom Sheehan ~

Hardly with a hop, skip and a jump did Frank Parkinson come home from Tobruk, Egypt, North Africa, madness, and World War II in general. A lot of pit stops were made along the way where delicate-handed surgeons and associates did their very best to get him back into working order. From practically every vantage point thereafter, we never saw, facially or bodily, any scar, bunching of flesh or major or minor skin disturbance. No permanent redness, no welts on his features, no thin and faintly visible testaments to a doctor's faulty hand or to the enemy's angry fragmentation. It was as if he were the ultimate and perfect patient, the great recovery, the risen Lazarus.

But he was different, it was easy to see, by a long shot.

Parkie. Tanker. Tiger of Tobruk.

And it was at the end of some trying times for him when I realized, one afternoon as we sat looking over the sunlit Lily Pond, a redness on the pond's face as bright as a pal's smile, the pond face we had skated on for almost twenty years, where we had whipped the long, hand-held whip line of us and our friends screaming and wind-blown toward the frosted shore on countless coffee-and-cider evenings, that he had come home to die.

The September sun was on for a short stay, and we had bagged a dozen bottles of beer and laid them easily down in the pond, watching the flotilla of pickerel poking slowly about when the sediment settled, their thin, elongated shadows pointing, like inert submarines or torpedoes, at the bags.

Our differences were obvious, though we did not speak of them. The sands of North Africa had clutched at him and almost taken him. Off a mountain in Italy I had come with my feet nearly frozen, graceless pieces of marble under skin, thinking they might have been blown off at the same quarry in which Michelangelo had once farmed torsos. Searching for the grace that might have been in them, I found none. I kept no souvenirs, especially none of Italy and its craggy mountains, and had seen nothing of Parkie's scenery momentoes. But once I saw a pair of tanker goggles hanging like an outsized Rosary on the post of Parkie's bed at Dutch Siciliano's garage where he roomed on the second floor. In each of his three small rooms, like the residue of a convoy's passing still hanging in the air, I could smell oil and grease and, sometimes I'd swear, acid-like cosmoline and spent gunpowder rising right through the floorboards.

We left the war behind us, as much as we could. But with Parkie it was different…pieces of it hung on as if they were on for the long ride. I don't mean that he was a flag waver or mufti hero now that he was out of uniform, but the whole war kept coming back to him in ways over which he had no control. There are people upon whom such things befall. They don't choose them, but it's as if they somehow get appointed to bear all the attendant crap that comes with life.

Furthermore, Parkie had no control over the visitations.

I don't know how many times we've been sitting in the Angels' Club, hanging out, the big booms long gone, when someone from Parkie's old outfit showed up out of the blue. Like Lamont Cranston appearing from the shadows, a guy would be standing at the door looking in and we'd all notice him, and then his eyes and Parkie's would lock. Recognition was instant; reaction was slower, as if neither believed what he was seeing.

There would be a quiet acceptance of the other's presence; they'd draw their heads together and have a beer in a corner. Parkie, as sort of an announcement, would speak to no one in particular and the whole room in general, "This guy was with me in North Africa." He never gave a name.

All of them were odd lots, all of them: thin like Parkie, drawn in the face, little shoulders and long arms, nervous, itchy, wearing that same darkness in the eyes, a sum of darkness you'd think was too much to carry. They would hang on for days at a time, holing up some place, sometimes at Parkie's and sometimes elsewhere, drinking up a storm, carousing, and then one morning the guy would be gone and never seen again, as if a ritual had taken place—a solemn ritual. Apparitions from the slippery darkness! Dark-eyed. The nameless out of North Africa and whatever other places they had been to and come back from. Noble wanderers, but nameless, placeless itinerants from who knows what.

Parkie never got a card or letter from any one of them, never a phone call. Nothing. He never mentioned them after they were gone. That, to me, was notice he knew they would never be back. It was like a date had been kept, a vow paid off. It wasn't at all like "We'll meet at Trafalgar Square after the war, or Times Square, or under the clock at The Ritz." Not at all. The sadness of it hit me solidly, frontally. I'd had some good buddies, guys I'd be tickled to death to see again if they walked in just like his pals did, and I knew that I'd never see *them* again. Things were like that, cut and dried like adobe, a place and a job in the world. And you couldn't cry about it. Part of the fine-tuned fatalism that grows in your bones, becomes part of you, core-deep, gut-deep.

The sun's redness on Lily Pond shivered under breeze. Pickerel nosed at the bags. The beer cooled. Parkie sipped at a bottle, his eyes dark, locked on the pond, seeing something I hadn't seen, I suppose. The long, hatchet-like face, the full-blown Indian complexion he owed great allegiance to, made his dark visage darker than it might have been. With parted lips his teeth showed long and off-white or slightly yellowed, sharp incisors in a deep-red gum line. On a smooth, gray rock he sat with his heels jammed up under his butt, the redness still locked in his eyes, and, like some long-gone Chief, locked in meditation of the spirits.

For a long while he was distant, who knows where, in what guise and in what act, out of touch, which really wasn't that unusual with him before, and surely wasn't now, since his return. Actually it appeared a little eerie, this sudden transport, but a lot of things had become eerie with Parkie around. He didn't like being indoors for too long a stretch. He craved fresh air and walked a lot and must have worn his own path around the pond. It went through the alders, then through the clump of birch that some nights looked like ghosts at attention, then down along the edge where all the kids went for kibby and sunfish, then over the knoll at the end of the pond where you'd go out of sight for maybe five minutes of a walk. Then finally down along the near shore and coming up to the Angels' where we hung out.

Most of the guys said when you couldn't find Parkie, you knew where to find him.

He looked up at me from his crouch, the bottle in his hand catching the sun, but his eyes as dark as ever in their deep contrast. "Remember that Kirby kid, Ellen Kirby, when we pulled her out of the channel on Christmas vacation in her snowsuit and she kept skating around the pond for a couple of hours, afraid to go home. We saved her for nothing, it seems, but for another try at it. I heard she drowned in a lake in Maine January of the year we went away. Like she never learned anything at all."

Parkie hadn't taken his eyes off the pond, stillness still trying to take hold of him, and he sipped and sipped and finally drank off the bottle and reached into the water for another. The pickerel force moved away as quickly as minnows. Their quickness seemed to make fun of our inertia.

If there was a clock handy, I knew its hands would be moving, the ticking going on, but I couldn't bet on it. We seemed to be holding our collective breath; the sun froze itself on the water's face, the slightest breath of wind held its passing. I heard no ticking, no bells, no alarms, and sudden disturbances in the air, no more war, and no passage of time. For a moment we hung at breathlessness and eternity. We were, as Parkie had said on more than one occasion, "Down-in deep counting the bones in ourselves, trying to get literate."

"We just got her ready to die another time." The church key opener in his hand pried at the bottle cap as slow as a crowbar and permitted a slight "pop," and he palmed the cap in his hand and shook it like half a dice set and skipped it across the redness. The deliberate things he did came off as code transmissions, and I had spent hours trying to read what kind of messages they carried along. They did not clamor for attention, but if you were only barely alert you knew something was cooking in him.

"You might not believe it," I said, "but I thought of her when I was in the base hospital in Italy and swore my ass was ice. I remember how she skated around after we pulled her out with that gray-green snowsuit on and the old pilot's cap on her head and the flaps down over her ears and the goggles against her eyes and the ice like a clear, fine lacquer all over her clothes. I thought she was going to freeze standing upright on the pond."

Parkie said, "I used to think about the pond a lot when I was in the desert, at Tobruk, at Al Shar-Efan, at The Sod Oasis, at all the dry holes along the way, but it was always summer and fishing and swimming and going balliky off the rock at midnight or two or three in the morning on some hot-ass August night when we couldn't sleep and sneaked out of the house. Remember how Gracie slipped into the pond that night and slipped out of her bathing suit and hung it up on a spike on the raft and told us she was going to teach us everything we'd ever need to know." His head nodded two or three times, accenting its own movement, making a grand pronouncement, as if the recall was just as tender and just as complete as that long-ago compelling night. He sipped at the bottle again and tried to look through its amber passage, dark eyes meeting dark obstacles. Much as a fortuneteller he looked, peeking into life.

All across the pond stillness made itself known, stillness as pure as any I've known. I don't know what he saw in the amber fluid, but it couldn't have been anything he hadn't seen before.

When I called him *Frank* he looked at me squarely, thick black brows lifted like chunks of punctuation, his mouth an *Oh* of more punctuation, both of us suddenly serious. It had always been that way with us, the reliance on the more proper name to pull a halt to what was about us, or explain what was about us. He drank off a heavy draught of beer, his Adam's apple flopping on his thin neck. The image of a turkey wattle came uneasily to mind. *Frank* was an announcement of sorts, a declaration that a change, no matter whether subtle or not, was being introduced into our conversation. It was not as serious as *Francis* but it was serious enough.

His comrades from North Africa, as always, intrigued me, and on a number of instances I had asked him for stories that might lie there waiting to get plowed up. Nothing I turned over, however, came anywhere close to the reality of terrors I had known in my own stead. No rubble. No chaff. No field residue.

Perhaps Parkie had seen something in that last bottle, something swimming about in the amber liquid, or something just on the other side of it, for he turned to me and said, "I think you want to know about my friends who visit, my friends from North Africa, from my tank outfit. I never told you their names because their names are not important. Where they come from or where they are going is not important, either. It would mean nothing to you."

Across the stretch of water the sun was making its last retreat of the day. A quick reflection of red light hung for a bare second on the face of the pond and then leaped off somewhere as if shot, past the worm-curled roots, a minute but energized flash darting into the trees. Then it was gone, absolutely gone, none of it yet curling round a branch or root, and no evidence of it lying about…except for the life it had given sustenance to, had maintained at all levels. It was like the shutter of a camera had opened and closed at its own speed.

Parkie acknowledged that disappearance with a slight nod of his head. An additional twist was there: it was obvious he saw the darkness coming on even before it gathered itself to call on us, as though another kind of clock ticked for him, a clock of a far different dimension. He was still chipping away at what had been his old self. That came home clean as a desert bone; but where he was taking it all was as much mystery as ever.

The beer, though, was making sly headway, the beer and stillness, and the companionship we had shared over the years, the mystery of the sun's quick disappearance on what we knew of the horizon, the thin edge of warmth it left behind, and all those strange comrades of his who had stood in the doorway of the Angels' Club, framed by the nowhere they had come from, almost purposeless in their missions. They, too, had been of dark visage. They too were lank and thin and narrow in the shoulder. They, too, were scored by that same pit of infinity locked deeply in their eyes. They were not haggard, but they were deep. I knew twin brothers who were not as close to their own core the same way these men were, men who had obviously leaned their souls entirely on some element common to their lives. I did not find it as intense even with battle brothers who had lain in the same hole with me while German 76ers slammed overhead and all around us chunks of grand Italian marble flew in awful trajectories.

The flotilla of pickerel nosed against the bags of beer. Parkie's

Adam's apple bobbed on his thin neck. He began slowly, all that long reserve suddenly beginning to fall away: "We were behind German lines, but had no idea how we got there. We ran out of gas in a low crater and threw some canvas against the sides of the three tanks that had been left after our last battle. If we could keep out of sight, sort of camouflaged, we might have a chance. It got cold that night. We had little food, little water, little ammo, and no gas. It was best, we thought, to wait out our chances. If we didn't know where we were, perhaps the Jerries wouldn't know, either. Sixteen of us were there. We had lost a lot of tanks, had our butts kicked."

He wasn't dramatizing anything. You could tell. It was coming as straight as he could make it.

"We woke up in the false dawn and they were all around us. Fish in the bottom of the tank is what we were. No two ways about it. Plain, all-out fish lying there, as flat as those pickerel. They took us without a shot being fired. Took us like babies in the pram. All day they questioned us. One was an SS guy, a real mean son of a bitch if you ever met one. Once I spit at him and he jammed me with a rifle barrel I swear six inches deep. Ten times he must have kicked me in the guts. Ten times! I couldn't get to his throat, I'd've taken him with me. They stripped our tanks, what was left, and that night they pushed us into them. I saw the flash of a torch through one of the gun holes. You could hear a generator working nearby. Something was crackling and blistering on the hull or the turret top. Blue light jumped every which way through the gun holes. It was getting hot. Then I realized the sounds and the smells and the weird lights were welding rods being burned. The sons of bitches were welding us inside our own tanks. A hell of a lot of arguing and screaming was going on outside. The light went flashing on and off, like a strobe light. Blue and white. Blue and white. Off and on. Off and on. But no real terror yet. Not until we heard the roar of a huge diesel engine. And the sound of it getting louder. And then came scraping and brushing against the sides of our tanks. Sand began to seep through the gun holes and peep sights. The sons of bitches were burying us in our own tanks! All I could see was that rotten SS bastard smiling down at us. I saw his little mustache and his pale green eyes and his red nose and a smile the devil must have created. And his shining crow-black boots."

I couldn't talk. A stunned sensation swept clean through me. Then disbelief, a surging block of disbelief, as if my veins had frozen in place. The dark pit in his eyes I saw was the darkness inside the tank, the utter, inhuman darkness that had become part of Parkie and part of his comrades. I knew a sudden likeness to that feeling: peering over the edge of a high place, the ground rushing up to meet me and then falling away and the long descent, the torturous fall becoming part of me…in the veins, in the mind. A shiver ran through every part of my body. And then hate welled up in me, stark, naked, unadorned hate, hate of the vilest kind.

Parkie put his hand on my knee. His grip was hard. "I never wanted to tell you, none of you. We all had our thing. You had yours. I had mine. I'm so sorry your feet are so screwed up. I wish nothing had happened to you. But a lot of guys've had worse."

"What happened?" I said, letting his hand carry most of his message, letting my own small miseries fall away. There was no comparison. My feet had iced up in my sleep. I knew the ignoble difference between that and burial.

"When the sand was almost over the entire tank, the noise started inside the tank. Screaming and cursing and crying. Cries like you never heard in your life. God-awful cries. I know I never heard anything like them. And coming out of guys I'd known a long time, tough guys, valiant guys, guys with balls who had gone on the line for me. I heard some of them call for their mothers. There was screaming, and then whimpering and then screaming again. And curses! My God, curses that would raise the friggin' dead. The most unholy of curses. Everything dead and unholy and illegitimate, raised from wherever, was brought against the Germans and that little SS bastard. He was castrated and ripped and damned and denounced to the fires of hell. You have not heard profanity and terror and utter and absolute hatred all in one voice at the same time. It filled the tank. It filled that makeshift vault. And our useless and agonized banging barehanded against the hull of the tank. Knuckles and fists and back-handers against the steel. But the outside noise drowned it all out."

I was still reeling, shaking my head, feeling the same glacier-like ice in my veins. And the heat of hatred coexisted with that ice. I was a mass of contradictions. Parkie kept squeezing my knee. The pickerel kept nosing the bags, hung up in their own world of silence. Silence extended itself to the whole of Earth. The *quiet out there*, the final and eventual *quiet out there*, after the war, was all around us.

"Suddenly," he continued, "there was nothing. The sand stopped its brushing and grating against the steel of the tank, then the diesel noise grew louder, as if it was coming right through us. And powerful thrusts came banging at the tank. I didn't know what it was. And then we were being shoved and shaken, the whole structure. And I heard curses from outside and a lot of German on the air, and we seemed to be moving away from our hole in the ground. Whatever it was was *pushing* at us. And then it went away and we heard the same banging and grinding and grunting of the engine nearby. Then the blue and white light again as a torch burned around us and the tank heated up, and lots of screaming but all of it German. And there were more engine noises and more banging and smashing of big bodies of steel. Finally the turret was opened and we were hauled out and canteens shoved in our faces and the other tanks were being opened up and guys scrambling out, some of them still crying and screaming and cursing everything around them."

He reached for the last bottle in one of the bags. The bag began to drift slowly away in wavy pieces. The pickerel had gone. The bottle cap snapped off in his hand. I thought of the tank's turret top being snapped open, the rush of clean air filling his lungs, a new light in his eyes.

"Then I saw him," Parkie said. "The minute I saw him I knew who he was. General Rommel. He was looking at us. He looked me right in the eye, straight and true and bone-steady and no shit at all in it. I didn't think he was breathing, he was so still. But I read him right off the bat. The whole being of that man was right in his eyes. He shook his head and uttered a cry I can't repeat. Then he took a pistol from another guy, maybe his driver, a skinny, itchy little guy, and just shot that miserable SS son of a bitch right between the eyes as he stood in front of him. Shot him like he was the high executioner himself; no deliberation, no second thought, no pause in his movement. Bang! One shot heard round the world if you really think about it. He screamed something in German as if it were at the whole German army itself, each and every man of it, perhaps rising to whatever god he might have believed in because it was so loud, so unearthly, and then he just walked off toward a personnel carrier, not looking at us anymore or the SS guy on the ground, a nice-sized hole in his forehead."

He drained off the last bottle, mouthing the taste of it for a while, wetting his lips a few times, remembering, I thought, the dry sands, the heat, the furious German general walking away on the desert, the graveyard for so many men, the graveyard for so many dreams.

"They gave us water and food, the Germans did. One of them brought up one of our own jeeps. It was beat to hell, but it was working. One German major, keeping his head down, his eyes on the sand, not looking at us, pointed off across the sand. We started out, the sixteen of us, some walking, some riding, some still crying or whimpering. Some still cursing. The next day we met some Brits. They brought us to their headquarters company. We were returned to our outfit. Some guys, of course, didn't get to go back on line, but were sent home as head cases. Can't blame them for that. I kept thinking about General Rommel, kept seeing his eyes in my mind. I can see them now, how they looked on his face, the shame in them. It was absolute, that shame, and he knew we knew. It was something he couldn't talk about, I bet. If he could have talked to us, we might have been taken to one of their prison camps. But he knew he couldn't do that to us. Make amends is what he had to do. He had to give us another chance. Just like we gave Ellen Kirby another chance at drowning."

In his short flight he had circled all the way back to the Kirby circumstance and all that played with it.

Francis Dever Parkinson, tanker sergeant, survivor of Tobruk and other places in the horrors of Northern Africa, who walked away from death in the sand on more than one occasion, who might be called Rommel's last known foe, who rolled over three cars on U.S. Route 1 and waged six major and distinct bouts with John Barleycorn thereafter in his time, who got to know the insidious trek of cancer in his slight frame, whom I loved more than any comrade that had shared a hole with me, who hurt practically every day of his life after his return from Africa, hung on for twenty-five more torturous and tumultuous and mind-driven years. They found him one night at the far end of the pond after he had gone missing for two days. I saw a handful of damp earth squeezed in one fist and thought perhaps Parkie was telling me it was better than the sand of the Sahara, that which he had traversed before being cast with his comrades into the crypt-like horror of the tank so many years ago, under the gaze of Africa's two dark eyes.

War Never Dies
Maroula Blades

It is the dread season,
the harvest of war
commences
where men thrash
bones for blood.
A barrage of bullets
pit flesh like a
battalion of hornets,
piercing in the
milk-mist of sober mornings.

The dead lie, as if
fallen fatally from trees
like fusty fruit,
numerous in weight,
piled one by one,
on top of hundreds.
There are no crates to
cart corpses to sorting
rooms for tagging.
The earth washes and claims.
Perhaps, the wind's sling
carries the dust of
loved ones home to rest.

Bleeding has stopped,
dim eyes gape in the
glare of a demi-veiled sun.
Worms wriggle in
and out of outdated rations,
as sun-shadows saunter
the seedless ground.
Air is shell-shocked.
A crater smokes,
in it, a child's leg.

A black patent shoe is
all that remains intact.

White frills from a
favourite frock, dresses
a hawthorn hedge
along a silent
blood-speckled path.
A tricycle lays twisted,
white wheels stained red.
The metal skeleton
given up to waste, punctured,
ditched among brambles.

Larks circle the sky;
it is brazenly blue.
Ten miles west,
landmines part the soil.

THE ENEMY

~ Michail Mulvey ~

This story is based on an eyewitness account by the author

He sat there in the dirt under a brutal sun, blindfolded, hands tied behind his back, barefoot, covered with muck and mud, and wearing only dirty black shorts, the same shorts I'd seen on a hundred other Vietnamese peasants. He could have been just one of the many innocent rice farmers we passed on our way out here, out in the middle of nowhere—'Search and Destroy' the Army called what we did, day after friggin' day.

Or he could be the enemy.

"They caught him not far from where that Alpha Company track ran over a mine. Fucker probably planted it," said the sergeant guarding him.

He could have been the same guy who planted that mine I ran over last month, or the guy who put an RPG in the gun shield of our track that day, or the sniper who shot my friend in the head . . . or he could be just an innocent civilian who happened to be in the wrong place at the wrong time.

Many of these same people, the ones we came here to help, smile as we pass. Others stare, stone-faced. Some glare with hate in their eyes, which puzzles the new guys. But this one, this dirty, ragged, nearly naked peasant, was suspected of being a Viet Cong. On one level, he was just a small cog in the big Cong machine. On a personal level, he was my enemy, one of the little people who snipe at me by day, mortar me at night, and plant mines for me to run over. And if he and his comrades have overwhelming firepower and numbers, they try to clean our clocks—kill us all, me included.

After I got here I heard stories, some true, some not, about how prisoners and suspects were interrogated. Heard a story early on about how three VC prisoners were taken up in a Huey and asked some questions. When the first one refused to answer, he was tossed out. The other two talked like there was no tomorrow. For the suspect given the free flying lessons, there was no tomorrow. At least that's what I heard.

This suspect sat there quietly, waiting outside the battalion operations center in the middle of our firebase. He must have been scared shitless. I would have filled my skivvies many times over if I'd been in his boots . . . or sandals. Blindfolded, he couldn't see what was going on around him. He could, though, hear the sounds of Hueys and Chinooks coming and going, the boom of outgoing artillery, vehicles, men shouting orders in a strange language, boots coming his way, stopping, then moving on. The uncertainty would have killed me, not knowing what was next.

I was thinking this guy must be thirsty sitting there under that sun, but SOP, Standing Operating Procedure, said prisoners get no water, at least not right away. They might be more willing to talk when they got real thirsty, or so it was thought. I had my doubts. I'd learned real quickly that these people were tough sons of bitches.

Danny had sent me to Supply to pick up some batteries for our radio. When I passed by the TOC—The Battalion Operations and Intel Bunker—I saw this guy sitting there in the dirt, all tied up, so I stopped to get a look at one of those little people who had been trying to kill me for the last sixty-eight days. Wasn't often we saw the enemy up close, if at all. Saw dead ones, the ones whose luck just up and ran out, or the slow and stupid ones. They got ripe real quick, the unlucky bastards and the slow and stupid ones, lying there out in the hot sun, a vacant look in their lifeless eyes, an arm or leg missing, their life's blood pooled next to them on the ground.

I stood off to the side like I had business there. Didn't want to be shooed away by officers or NCO's from what I thought was about to happen. Like I said, I'd heard stories. I didn't envy him as he sat there, waiting for his interrogators. No sir. Wouldn't want to be in his shoes—but he wasn't wearing any. I had a feeling this particular local might be in for a long day.

Just as I was starting to lose interest—it was hot and it was getting on to noon—along came the battalion S-2, our intelligence officer, and our Vietnamese interpreter, a tall, skinny ARVN staff sergeant: ARVN, Army of the Republic of Vietnam. Our allies. The people we came here to help.

Our S-2 was a fat-faced captain with eyes like two peas sitting in a heaping plate of mashed potatoes, hidden behind black-framed Army-issue glasses. His starched and pressed uniform was soaked in sweat. "This pale-faced fucker would probably sweat in a friggin' blizzard," I muttered under my breath. His gut pressed against the buttons of his uniform, endangering anyone who got too close, especially in the mess hall when he shoveled pork chops, mashed potatoes and ice cream into his cakehole. Judging by his pale face and arms, and his clean uniform, he probably hadn't spent much time in the field. Hard to get a tan sitting on a barstool at the Officer's Club back at base camp.

I'd heard a story about how this fat S-2 sent an ambush patrol from the recon platoon out one night and they walked into the kill zone of an ambush set up by our allies, the ARVNs. There were dead and wounded on both sides. Of course the fat fuckin' S-2 tried to blame the patrol leader for not reading the map right—"Had the wrong grid coordinates," he said, or so I heard. Bullshit. I wondered how many men had stepped in it using this S-2's faulty intel.

Before the two of them went to work on the suspect, the S-2 briefed the ARVN sergeant, telling him what information he needed from the guy. First thing the ARVN did was walk over to the suspect, yell at him, and kick the guy in the leg, hard. The suspect screamed in pain and rolled over on his side. He had no clue that those feet he heard coming his way were meant for him. The ARVN sergeant yelled at him again, the veins in his neck bulging out. The suspect answered in a whiney, pleading voice, probably telling the ARVN sergeant he wasn't VC. The sergeant kicked him again, this time in the ribs. The suspect cried out again, babbling something in Vietnamese. Then the sergeant picked the suspect up by the neck and arm, squeezing the guy's neck as he lifted him, digging his fingers in. The ARVN looked pissed, or maybe that was just part of the game. The ARVN held him in an iron grip while he yelled at him once more, his mouth just a few inches from the suspect's ear.

Since he was blindfolded, the suspect didn't see the fist that caught him right in the middle of the blindfold, probably breaking his nose. Must hurt twice as much when you can't see it coming. It also sent the suspect flying, setting him on his ass once more. Again the ARVN picked the guy up by the neck, all the while shouting in his ear. The ARVN punched him once more, again, right in the middle of the blindfold. I'd seen fights before, guys getting the shit knocked out of them, but this poor fucker was blindfolded and tied up. Not even close to a fair fight. But this was war.

The suspect was babbling something, half pleading, half crying as he lay on the ground, blood dripping down from under his blindfold onto his mouth and chin. The ARVN picked him up again, squeezing his neck and screaming into his face. All this time the S-2 just stood there, watching. Occasionally he would, in a quiet voice, pass along another question to the sergeant. The fat captain just watched, a thoughtful look on his face, like he was thinking of more questions: "Ask where the weapons are hidden, who is his commander?" he calmly told the sergeant. The sergeant nodded to the captain, turned and resumed the interrogation. This was beginning to look like one of those interrogations I'd seen in the movies, where the Nazis are beating on some French Resistance guy or something.

It wasn't a pleasant sight, truth be told, and I was about to walk away, disgusted. I was starting to get pissed at this ARVN sergeant. It must have been against the Geneva Convention to beat the shit out of this guy, I was thinking, but the fat captain covered his pasty white ass and got around this legal technicality—no doubt worked out by other fat, pasty-faced men in suits, twelve thousand miles away in another time zone—by having the ARVN sergeant ask the questions.

I can't say I was surprised at the brutality of the ARVN sergeant, though. Before I arrived in-country I'd seen pictures in *Life* magazine about how the ARVNs interrogated peasants suspected of being VC. They'd beat the shit out of them for starters, then tie them up and hold them under water for a while, then pull them up and ask a couple of simple questions. If the suspect—many times an innocent villager—didn't tell the ARVNs what they wanted to hear, they gave him some more swimming lessons. If the swimming lessons didn't work, they'd start to cut him open until the peasant spilled his guts, one way or the other. If the ARVNs were really pissed, had lost some men to sniper fire coming from the village in question, they'd sometimes just out-and-out shoot the guy. Then they'd rape the women, burn their thatched houses, and steal their pigs and chickens. Brutal. Their own people. I was guessing the ARVNs probably converted more peasants to the Commie cause than all the VC political cadres combined.

As I stood there, my mind went back to one Memorial Day long ago. A friend of my Uncle Bob, a guy named Tim, was dressed in his Marine Corps uniform, a member of the color guard that led a long parade of veterans, a company from the local National Guard armory, cops, firemen and boy scouts, to the war memorial on Main Street. He stood stiffly at attention, M-1 on his shoulder while the mayor made a long and boring speech, something about patriotism and sacrifice. I couldn't take my eyes off Tim and the others in uniform, all standing tall in the spring sun. I knew my uncle had been in the Korean War, but I had never seen him in his Marine uniform before.

After all the speeches were done, men from the color guard and several other veterans in the parade came over to our apartment for beer and sandwiches. I stood off to the side and listened as my Uncle Bob, bottle of beer in hand, traded stories with his buddies, some in Navy blues, others in Army brown. Tim had been wounded by a grenade, my uncle told me as we stood in the kitchen. Tim's face was pocked and he wore thick glasses, the result of that grenade going off just outside his frozen foxhole.

"Sometimes, when we were ordered to bring some gook prisoners back to battalion, we'd walk them down the road a bit, then shoot 'em. It was cold and too far to walk. We told the lieutenant they tried to escape." His comment made no impression on me at the time. War is war. I'd seen war movies at the drive-in and on TV. *To Hell and Back*, starring Audie Murphy, was my favorite.

But it was one thing to watch movies or listen to stories and another to see it first-hand, up close. I felt something turn in my stomach. I decided I had seen enough, but just as I was about to leave, an American sergeant walked up to the fat captain. The sergeant was carrying a TA-312, an Army field phone. The sergeant had a tired, disinterested, 'I-don't-give-a-shit' look on his face like he'd seen this all before.

When we were dug in, the TA-312s were connected together by long lines of black, double-strand commo wire. The 312 saved on radio batteries and was a more secure way of communication. When you wanted to talk to someone, you'd use a little hand crank on the side to send a current down the wire where a buzzing sound told the guy on the other end to answer the phone. It's about the size of one of your Aunt Martha's pound cakes, comes in a green canvas case, and has a handset that looks just like the receiver on your phone back home.

The American sergeant tried to hand the TA-312 to the fat captain, but the fat captain pointed to the ARVN sergeant. The ARVN took the TA-312, placed it on the ground, attached some commo wire to it, then wrapped the other, bare ends of the wire to the big toes of the poor bastard lying there in the dirt who was probably wondering what was going on. But he couldn't see shit with that blindfold and all.

The captain finally noticed my standing there, holding those two batteries with an uneasy, questioning look on my face, but I quickly looked off into the distance like I wasn't paying any attention to this so-called 'interrogation.' I acted like I was just waiting on someone from the TOC.

The ARVN picked up the TA-312 and grabbed hold of the hand crank. He asked the suspect a couple more questions, this time in a calm, almost soothing voice, like he was giving the guy one more chance to save his ass. The suspect babbled something, probably telling the ARVN he was just a poor farmer with a family and that he was on his way from point A to point B when he was collared by the Americans. The ARVN stood up and yelled something, probably telling him he's full of shit, that he's a fuckin' VC, and that if he doesn't talk he's gonna die, or worse, die slowly.

This poor rice farmer said something, but he wasn't babbling or crying now. He sounded desperate, really fuckin' scared. He was still blindfolded, not knowing what was coming next, probably wondering about those wires wrapped around his big toes. Or maybe he knew what was coming. The ARVN started cranking on that TA-312 like crazy, sending one hell of a charge down those wires. You should have seen that 'sumbitch bounce along the ground on his ass as the ARVN cranked that TA-312. The little guy in black was yelling and bouncing, bouncing and yelling, and all the while the ARVN sergeant was smiling, an evil smile, like he was having fun. He stopped cranking and whispered something to the guy, probably something like "I told you bad things would happen if you didn't answer my questions truthfully."

I knew first hand that it hurt like a motherfucker, having that electrical charge run through your body, in his case, up his toes and his legs to who knows where. If you were new in-country and to the company or you just looked stupid—I must have been all of the above—the commo guys would sometimes ask you to help them out for a second: "Hold these two wires for me, would ya, while I connect this fucker to battalion." While you're holding the two wires, they'd crank up the TA-312 and laugh their asses off while you screamed and jumped as the current ran up your arms.

While the little man sitting in the dirt was being interrogated, other guys in my company walked by. Some stopped for a moment to watch. Most just walked on by like they'd seen it before. Or maybe they didn't want to know what was going on. Didn't want to get involved. Or just didn't give a shit 'cause they'd been here too long and nothing surprised them anymore. None of the passers-by said a word or betrayed any emotion that I could see.

The ARVN sergeant asked more questions—or maybe he asked the same ones over and over—I couldn't tell, I didn't speak the language. "Didi mau" and "Xin loi" was the limit of my expertise in the local lingo. This poor bastard was yakking away at a million miles an hour now, but he must not have been telling the ARVN sergeant what he wanted to hear because the sergeant cranked on that TA-312 some more, so hard he was working up a good sweat.

I watched this for a while, watched the suspect bounce along the ground, screaming and thrashing about while the ARVN smiled and the fat captain stood there, watching, arms crossed, a thoughtful look on his face. I might have even detected a slight look of amusement on his fat mug. I was starting to feel sorry for this poor guy bouncing along in the dirt, blindfolded and tied up . . . even though he could be my enemy. Even though he might have been the one who planted the mine I ran over last month . . . even though he might have been the one who shot my friend in the head . . . even so . . . .

I wanted to go over and kick the ARVN sergeant's balls up around his ears . . . even though he's on our side and one of those people we came here to help. I remembered this particular sergeant now. Saw him walking out of the NCO Club one night, glassy-eyed, drooling, tripping over rocks, real and imagined. He always seemed to be drunk, now that I thought of it, and he was always trying to borrow money from the American NCOs. That red glow he had on his face was booze burn. Had nothing to do with the sun.

Our allies.

What I wanted to do even more was punch that fat captain in his fuckin' jaw. I didn't care for most officers anyway, but this fat fuck, he was just standing there, calmly passing questions to the ARVN, watching him crank on that TA-312, not getting his hands dirty. His conscience was clean: "I'm just asking the questions. The ARVN is doing the interrogating."

I walked away. PFCs don't give orders to captains. And if you punch an officer, any officer, even fat, pasty-faced captains, you land in Leavenworth. When I got back to our bunker, Danny had just finished cleaning his weapon. I dropped the batteries on the ground and told him what I'd just witnessed, but he didn't even look up. He told me he'd seen worse but provided no details. I didn't want any details, I'd seen all I wanted to see. I was guessing he'd been here too long and had other things on his mind, like his DEROS, his Date of Expected Return from Overseas. Danny was short. "Change the battery and do a commo check," he said, tapping a new magazine into his M-16.

Terry walked over and asked if I saw the suspect being interrogated.

"Yeah," I told him. "I'm glad I'm not in his sandals." I felt more than sympathy, though. I wanted to say, "We're the good guys and we're not supposed to pull that shit, right?" But I was the FNG, the new guy, two hundred and ninety-seven days left, so I held my tongue.

"Isn't he the gook Alpha Company caught hiding in the bush near where one of their tracks ran over a mine?" Terry asked. "That little raggedy-ass motherfucker probably planted it." He spit into the dirt and shifted the M-16 to his other hand. Terry had an angry, worn and tired look on his face.

"But did you see that ARVN asshole beating the shit out of him while he was tied and blindfolded?" I asked.

"Yeah, I saw him. Remember what happened to guys in the First Cav up in the Ia Drang back in '65? The NVA didn't take any prisoners. Made 'em kneel, then shot them in the fuckin' face."

"Still . . . ."

"Still nothing. This guy's getting off easy. He's lucky Alpha Company didn't just smoke his ass right then and there. Besides, what he's getting is nothing," Terry said. "I heard from some advisors that the ARVNs attach alligator clips to the ends of the wires and then attach 'em to the guy's nuts. If it's a woman, they attach them clips to her nipples or worse." I didn't want to hear anymore. My knees involuntarily jerked together like they had been jolted by the TA-312, and my right hand involuntarily moved towards my left breast. Terry looked at me hard for a minute, spit in the dirt, then walked away.

"He's the enemy. He's trying to kill me," I said to myself. I opened a can of C's, stared at the congealed pork slices in the dark green can and threw it into the hole we used for our latrine. I took my M-16 and sat on our bunker, staring out at the distant wood line.

"He's the enemy," I said to myself again. "He's trying to kill me."

The Fear Muscles
Brandon Courtney

I.
Darwin's words resurface days after I've abandoned
his book—*when our minds are much affected,*

so are the movements of our bodies. Just days stateside,
I'm rummaging rifles, ammunition, and antique pistols

at a gun show in the hotel's grand pavilion, watching
a boy level the barrel of a Winchester at his younger

brother's chest—scarcely able to steady the carbine's
weight. Still, he must understand how delicately

his brother is tethered to this world. He shields his face
with both hands outstretched, turns away, flinching,

the body's only argument for life. He falls the way
he thinks soldiers fall, his palms clotting the phantom

wound, star-shaped, his slow plummet more crouch
than buckle, the hotel's floral carpet softly breaking

his body's momentum. I want to say no, a bullet
makes a man precisely aware of his body, aware

of the dusty Fallujah street—the vendors selling dried
figs, a chip of light glinting from razor-wire, aware of shots

fired during a wedding party, and those fired by a sniper.
But how does the boy know to keep his eyes closed, to lie

there motionless, holding his breath? Does he know
when the game is over; how does he know how to rise?

II.
In Basra, I steal away to the burn-out latrine, a Glock
holstered in my belt. I press blue steel to my mouth's

soft palate, bite down hard into the barrel, roll its metal
like communion on my tongue. I think of nothing;

I fall asleep, wake only when the gun slips from my hand.
Now, I swallow two teardrop pills to sleep, dream

a prescriptioned dream. Most nights I pull the trigger,
jerk awake to sounds my mind mistakes for the bullet's

sudden punch: shutters slapped against our pane, my lover's
hair brushed against my temple. Tomorrow, she'll tell

me of a soldier's wife found shot in the back
seat of her minivan, a gag of duct tape wreathing her head.

GHOST
~ Danny Johnson ~

The sun beat down hot as a baker's brick. Sweat ran down my arms and between my palms and the wooden grubbing hoe handle. The ground I hacked was hard as a three-day-old biscuit.

I was eighteen years old, with two years of school left, at least, and the only thing I knew how to do was grub potatoes and steal hogs. From the time I could walk good, I must have dug a million pounds. On our sorry ground farm in North Carolina, potatoes was about all we had to eat, that, collard greens, turnips, and mule corn. But every year around Christmas I walked with my daddy in the middle of the night two or three miles to one of the farms a good distance away. We sneaked down to the pigpen and daddy would whap one over the head with a baseball bat, drag her out, stick her in the neck, tie her legs over a tree limb, and we would tote her back. Once we set into that hog, there was nothing left but the smell and toenails. Him, Momma, and me ate pork until we all had a case of the worms. I wondered from time to time why nobody ever came looking for their hog.

I had no ambitions to farm the rest of my life and was sick to death of my circumstances, poor with no prospects of things getting any better. It felt like it was time for a change. The next morning I put on some clean overalls and a shirt, walked and thumbed to Raleigh, and asked until I found the military recruiter station. I went up to a Marine man. "Mister, my name is Ray Jacobs, and I want to sign up."

"When do you want to go in?" he asked.

"Today." I was through with living like a starving dog. At least in the Marines I figured we would get to eat on a regular basis.

"You want to call your parents and let them know?"

"Got no phone. They'll know I'm gone when I ain't home for supper."

"If you're sure that's what you want, we can make it happen."

On Tuesday July 12, 1960, I took the oath to join the United States Marine Corps. By Wednesday, I was at Parris Island, South Carolina, preparing for sixteen weeks of hell. It wasn't so bad, mostly hard work and a lot of yelling, but, man, did we eat good. I added twenty pounds to my six-foot frame pretty quick, and even made expert on the shooting range, guessing all those days hunting rabbits and squirrels wasn't for naught. I didn't make any fuss, just did what they told me and kept to myself mostly. All that hollering didn't bother me, neither did the marching, or any of the other shit the drill instructor made us do. The hand-to-hand combat was pretty fun, and I never did go against anybody whose ass I couldn't whup, probably because of grubbing all them potatoes.

In December, a group of us was sent to Camp Pendleton in California to get more training in assaulting beaches and different ways of how to stay alive in a war. At the end of March, 1961, they shipped us out to Camp Schwab in Okinawa, where we trained even more. There were starting to be barracks politics about this place called Viet Nam. Nobody really knew much about it, but it didn't keep them from starting rumors every day. I kept busy on the base during the day and at the bars at night. The Asian girls were pretty and cheap, and for an old country boy who'd never even been laid, life just didn't get much better.

The next year I got shipped back to California and was sent to see a psychiatrist who said he was going to do a personality test on me. I was assigned to sniper school the next month, so I guessed they didn't think I was crazy, and must have passed whatever they were testing me for.

We spent a lot of time training how to use a Winchester Model 70 .30-06 rifle and a Unerti scope. The instructors taught us how to allow for wind, humidity, distance, and a whole lot of other things I'd never thought about. What I enjoyed most was learning how to disguise and make myself invisible. I was good at that. The job was to work pretty much alone when they said you was ready, but first, you had to be a spotter for a regular sniper, learning under him about what it took to do the job.

After my four years were up in July of 1964, I re-enlisted, not bothering to go home on leave. There wasn't anything back there for me. In June, 1965, I was assigned to the 2nd Battalion, 3rd Marines, and we shipped out on a boat to Hawaii where we stayed a few weeks before going on to land in Da Nang, Vietnam. I was part of a Scout Sniper Team, something new to the Marines and not well regarded. Once there, I got sent to Hill 282, which was above DaNang and close to the DMZ. Our job was to keep the NVA from infiltrating to the South. It took a week to get settled in before I went out with a senior sniper everybody called Snake. He told me the old guard of the Marines didn't want us and really didn't give a shit what we did, so we made up a lot of our own missions and went to the bush to do what we had trained for. He said not to worry about getting killed because Marines guarded the Pearly Gates, and they always had room for one more brother. He let me make my first kill at a distance of three hundred yards, what he called a "confidence kill."

Thinking back on it, I don't know if it was a purpose target or just some poor guy that had the bad luck of wandering into range. Snake had a lot of combat experience from Korea, so I paid good attention to him. He was a big-jawed ol' boy from South Carolina, easy going and friendly. Every time we got ready to go into the bush, he'd say, "Come on, son, let's go put some meat on the ground." I never asked why they called him Snake or what his real name was. After a few missions he said I was as natural a sniper as he had ever been around.

"You know why?" he asked me.

"Because I like the aloneness of it?" To me that was the best part.

"That too, but it's because you never try to change circumstances, you just adapt to what is. That's a good trait for a sniper, and not a bad way to live your life." It took me a long time thinking, trying to figure out how he knew me that well. If a hole had water, I wouldn't try to bail it out, just sit and endure it.

He got serious with me for a minute. "Ray, you're starting down a road that's got a lot of bumps and gullies and it ain't paved. There's going to come a time in your life when you might wish you had took another way. You ain't never going to be the same."

I didn't really understand it at the time but it was something I never forgot.

The first time we went into the jungle at night, I knew I was home. Back on the farm, I had a habit of roaming the woods in the dark, able to sneak up on rabbits or squirrels, staying quiet and learning what natural animals do, plus they tasted mighty good with biscuits and gravy. In the jungle my sense of becoming invisible developed stronger, allowing me to vanish, become a shadow of the shadows. I had no fear being in the bush because it felt natural. The dark seemed to make me calm, like it was letting me know this was the place I would learn to taste life at its sweetest, and know death was insignificant.

"You know something, Ray, you can be one scary fucker. Most boys working out here in the jungle at night would be pissing in their pants at first, but you took to it like a duck to water. And you're good at it. I think I'll call you Ghost from now on."

I smiled at Snake, pleased I had earned a nickname. "This is going to sound crazy, Sergeant, but I think I've been training for this all my life."

The night belonged to me, and killing was a job, one with no remorse and no mercy required. Snake told me never to look the man I had to kill in the eyes, that way he'd never come visit me in my dreams, that they weren't people, just targets. I tried to do as he said, except the part about looking them in the eyes. I sealed in my brain the shock on every face when my bullet delivered. Sometimes spit would drool out of my mouth. It was a sense of absolute power I'd never known before. When it came to killing a man, there wasn't any real drama, they usually didn't holler and thrash around, just folded like a paper sack. It was mostly silent, deadly, and final.

In two months, I was cut loose from Snake, out every day, training a new guy to be a spotter, letting him learn from me. At first he was like Snake said, piss-in-his-pants scared. I tried to teach him patience and the secret of how to become invisible, but he never did catch on too good.

Sometimes we would hunt targets, laying in hiding for hours along trails. Other times we would go in ahead of ground assaults, having time to get positioned to support the regular force. We learned to live like animals, think like one, smell like one, with only one thing on our minds, killing. When we had the shot, everything jacked up; I could smell the scent of fear; the excitement in the air would sometimes actually give me an erection. Squeezing the trigger and watching the impact was as good as any orgasm I got from the whores around the village. We walked on the edge of the razor blade, knowing any slip would be fatal, and it was the most exhilarating sensation I'd ever felt. I was finally somebody other folks respected. And I was growing.

It did become lethal for Mo. It was the only name I ever called my spotter because I never wanted to know his real one. We had been dropped by helicopter into the A Shau Valley, and slipped up the south end close to Laos where the NVA operated openly, stockpiling stuff to be sent down the Ho Chi Minh Trail. We made our kill and had to inch along in mountainous cover for five hours to get to a place we could move quicker. NVA were all around us. About sundown, we came out of some elephant grass at a tree line. I was ten yards in back of Mo when I heard him cussing.

"Help me, Ghost!"

By the time I worked my way up, he was pale and having trouble breathing. Two puncture wounds were high on his right cheek.

"What was it, Mo? Did you see what kind it was?"

"Krait," he groaned.

We had been taught about snakes in the jungle, and the banded Krait was the worst of the worst. There was nothing I could do. He was going to choke to death because the poison attacked a person's nervous system. I went into my rucksack and got a sock. Mo was hurting bad and his face was swelling and changing to a sick yellow color. I stuck the sock in his mouth to quiet his moaning, and jabbed him with a morphine shot to ease the pain. "I'm going to sit here with you, Mo."

I wrapped my arms tight around him. He nodded, tears running down his face.

I rocked him like his momma would, whispering in his ear. "Mo, I want you to know that peace is coming and your pain will go away. It doesn't hurt when you die. You just go to sleep. Ain't nothing to be afraid of. That's what I want you to think about. In that instant you go from this life, you'll be in a better one. Don't mean nothing. I'm going to sit and hold you. You go ahead on when you're ready."

He was dead in ten minutes. I pulled his life force, the St. Christopher around his neck, and put it in my pocket. We all carried one kind or another. I rigged a stretcher; the thought of leaving him behind never crossing my mind. By the end of the second day, Mo was stinking something awful. On the third day, I got to a pick up LZ and a chopper lifted us out. I got Mo's address from the Chaplin and wrote his momma a letter.

> Dear Mrs. Morris:
> I wanted to let you know your son was a good man and
> brave soldier. You should know he didn't die alone. I
> held him until he was gone. His St. Christopher is here.
> I thought you might want it to remember him.
> Your friend,
> Ray Jacobs

At the end of my one-year tour, I had thirty-three kills I could document, and a bunch more I couldn't. The legend of the Ghost began to be whispered about, and regular grunts tended to avoid me. Something had indeed changed. Instead of just rubbing on black and green camouflage, I began to cut nicks in my arms and outline my face with patterns of red, trying to copy visions of ancient warriors that came to me in dreams, like they recognized a kindred soul.

I killed a vulture and wove its tail feathers into my hair, absorbing its powers of knowing death. Ray was disappearing, becoming hard for me to recognize or remember. In his place, a beast was growing. Each time I readied to go out, the taste in my mouth sweetened and my senses were honed so acute even the wind had a natural voice I could understand. I was evolving, becoming the breeze that moved the trees and elephant grass, a shadow in the darkness that slipped silently, confusing any eye that could be watching.

I refused the chance to rotate back to the States, and extended for another year. After Mo, I wouldn't train anybody else. Unless they gave me a specific job, I would slip into the bush, stay gone for two or three days, sometimes a week at a time, killing targets of opportunity. Nobody seemed to care, happy to avoid me and what I represented: the thing they were afraid they would become.

The Captain called me in one morning in October. "Jacobs, I've got a mission for you. You like to work alone so this should be right down your alley. If you fuck up, you'll be on your own. I'm telling you up front the Cavalry won't be coming."

He sat and stared over the table at me. I guess he was looking for a reaction. He didn't get one.

He showed me a map detailing a valley above the DMZ. "We think the gooks are building up in this area. We have reports of sightings of a white man working with an NVA regiment. The locals say he's an American, but we think he may be Russian, probably helping set up SAM sights in the mountains. We want you to find and eliminate him."

He sat back.

I studied the map for a few minutes. The territory had lots of open spaces between the hills. If I got caught on their side of the DMZ, death would be the easiest outcome I could expect. I pushed the map back to the Captain. "When do I leave?"

"You feel confident you can handle this?"

I leaned over towards him. He recoiled getting a whiff of my odor. "If I didn't think so, I wouldn't go."

"Get your stuff ready and we'll chopper you in after dark. You know you smell like shit don't you?"

I grinned, showing teeth that hadn't been brushed in a month. "Wouldn't have it any other way."

I stood up to leave. "Be seeing you." I had quit saluting assholes months before.

In my bunker, I rolled a joint to take the edge off, lay down on a cot and was asleep in minutes, knowing I would need the rest. It was a mental discipline practiced to perfection. Waking up around six in the afternoon, I stuffed my stomach with as much protein as I could, checked my gear and packed both side pockets with peanuts I'd bought from villagers. It was going to be a long mission and I didn't want to be loaded down with C-rats as extra weight. There was plenty to eat in the jungle.

At dark I headed to the helicopter field and found the Captain. He showed me to the chopper taking me across the DMZ. It was all black, no insignias, and the crew wore black, unmarked uniforms. Their faces were camouflaged and they carried two big fifties, one strapped to each open door, and a pod of rockets. These boys meant business. The Captain stepped back when the rotors began to stir. He threw me a salute, like he was in a John Wayne movie. I laughed as we lifted off and faded into the darkness.

We rode about two hours, low around the hills and through valleys. The sky was cloudy and gave good cover. The pilot signaled thumbs up, then dove for ground, pulling level just above tall elephant grass in a flat area. I threw on my rucksack, shouldered my rifle and jumped the final three feet to the ground. I'd barely hit good when the chopper was hauling ass. Immediately I moved five hundred yards towards a tree line in the distance. If the gooks had spotted the chopper, I didn't want to be sitting and waiting for them to come and have a look-see. When I got to good cover, I wrapped myself in grass and bushes, snuggling inside a high stand of bamboo. There I waited until first light so I could get my bearings and start moving.

At dawn, with the sun to my front, I began to walk, staying inside heavy jungle where possible, pausing and listening every few minutes. Steamy heat sucked the strength right out of a man, thorn bushes and razor-sharp elephant grass ripped skin, and every creek was loaded with leeches. Inconveniences, no surprises.

The NVA base camp was about four klicks, roughly two and a half miles through heavy jungle. Doing it the right way by avoiding trails and backtracking so I didn't have company would require two days to get there. By the second night, I came to the edge of a large open field of elephant grass dotted with bomb craters. I went up a big banyan tree to get some vision across, hoping I was in the right place. From that vantage point, lights from cooking fires and headlights of vehicles moving around beyond the end of the field told me it was what I'd been looking for. I dug clumps of grass, fixing them to my back, legs, helmet, and shoulders, then took my rifle, leaving the rucksack buried, and began to work my way into the field, trying to look as natural as possible. By morning, I had covered half the distance and could see the encampment clearly. I lay where I was to wait for night.

During the day, a lazy NVA patrol walked all around me, one guy stopping to piss so close I could smell his sour urine. I controlled my breathing and slowed my heart. The atmosphere was intense until they moved on. Things in the camp died down around midnight, and I moved quickly to a giant ant mound so as to have some cover and be high enough to see clearly. The peanuts gave me the energy to stay awake. They also worked on my bowels pretty hard, the other reason I kept them, so before sunup I had to scoot down a ways, cutting off a piece from the bottom of my fatigues to wipe with.

At dawn, sunlight crawled over the mountains to the east and started to roll down the valley. Activity in the camp soon followed. I watched through my scope, adjusting for wind and distance. It would be about a seven-hundred-yard shot. Soldiers squatted around, brewing tea and talking, no reason to be concerned this far north. No white man was visible. Then, a curtain moved on one of the hootches, and out he came. He stretched and yawned, lifting his cap to scratch his blond head. He was a big bastard, and I centered on the middle of the triangle between his armpits and his bellybutton; it was too far to risk a headshot. I couldn't tell if he was American or Russian, but that wasn't my job. My job was to kill him.

Letting out my breath, then waiting between one heartbeat and the next, I squeezed the trigger. The hat was still in his hand when he pitched backwards. I imagined the round blowing open his breastbone, tearing through his heart and turning it to jelly, then ripping apart his spine. His body twitched for a few seconds. The other soldiers froze where they were, in shock at what had happened. They went to jabbering, grabbing AK47s, and firing in all directions. It was obvious they didn't even know where the shot came from.

I began crawling as controlled as possible, moving quickly, but not to attract any attention. Slithering on my belly, I covered about a hundred yards before hearing vehicles coming to life and human noises moving my way. I sank into the red earth on the underside rim of a bomb crater, covering myself with dirt and mud, in my mind making my body invisible, my face buried into the ground, not daring a twitch.

NVA soldiers swarmed, shouting instructions, firing off weapons at anything that moved. I heard them going over the field like a colony of Army ants. But, by some miracle, they didn't find me. When night fell again, the sky clouded over and it began to rain, coming in buckets. The NVA moved on, leaving me the chance to cover the rest of the distance, recover my pack, and boogie.

The next day I was on the move south when I became aware a squad of gooks had somehow picked up my scent and were trailing me, keeping me from going to the pickup point. Tired of their bullshit, I backtracked and slipped up on their camp that night. I found a perimeter guard dozing, gagged him, and dragged him off. After interrogating him, he got across to me that the NVA had teams out hunting, and put up a big reward for anybody who could kill the Ghost. I took his rice and water, then sawed off his head with my K-Bar, stuck it on a bamboo pole, and left it on a trail his unit would travel.

It was fun matching wits with the little fucks, and I was in no hurry to get back to base camp. The greatest pleasure was hiding right in among them, then silently cutting a throat while the rest slept. I always left a wad of peanut hulls so they would know the Ghost had visited.

I was void of any emotions, thinking nothing more about killing a man than I would a gnat. After a week of hide-and-seek, I could smell their fear as easy as Momma's cornbread. They finally pulled off the pursuit and I was disappointed.

It was three weeks before I got back to the firebase. Other Marines avoided me. I didn't blame them. When I looked at a mirror in my bunker I scared myself. My face was drawn in weird angles and my eyes seemed to be fixed wide open from working so much in the dark. The blood stripes had liquefied and run down in ragged trails from my face to my neck. I wouldn't take a bath or rub off the camouflage. I reported back to the Captain the next morning, assuring him the job was done. He suggested I take some down time, and a bath. I told him I didn't need either one, and headed out again that night.

Three days later, I came in to resupply, slipping past the forward guard post, walking through the gate before anybody noticed. Early the next morning the Captain hauled me in. Him and the Chaplain sat me down to have a conversation about what I was doing, how I was fucking up big time. They insinuated I was over the edge.

"Jacobs, you're out of control. You just go and come as you please; I have no fucking idea where you are half the time. Hell, if you get killed out there, I wouldn't even know it. What the fuck are you thinking? You act like some kind of animal."

Things got silent, no incoming, no outgoing, just the whirring fan on his desk. I pulled my chair closer, letting him look into my eyes red from lack of sleep and whiff the stink of my body. Soap was out because I knew how well Charlie could smell. Once I saw he was getting it, I smiled to show my teeth, black from chewing betel nut to take the shine off.

"I am an animal," I growled, causing them to shift in their chairs. "Made by you. An animal you think you can keep tied to a tree, then unleash when you got shit nobody else has the balls to do. You think you can control me?" I spit on his dirt floor. "The only control you got is what I let you have. The Marine Corps sent me here so cherry I didn't know whether to shit or go blind. I was lucky to survive the first month. You wanted me to kill people, just run out there in the bush and start knocking them down. So simple for you to sit here and hide like a bunch of bitches. Well, I learned, and I learned good. Yeah, I'm an animal." I ran my finger down my face, tracing scars made of my own blood. "And I'm the king of this fucking jungle." I gripped the sides of the chair, my body and face so intense the two of them leaned back.

After a minute, I forced myself to relax, then lit up a joint, slowly sucking it in deep, watching them look at each other, trying to figure out how to react.

Everybody in the bush knew there was a line that if a man crossed it, better to kill him than let him back among civilized people. I had crossed it a long time ago. My mind was in a world to itself, the darkness in my soul fully exposed and unleashed; nothing else existed. I no longer knew who I was or who they were and the color of the uniform didn't matter. If I wanted you dead, you would be dead. "Nobody's give a damn this long, now you're suddenly concerned about my well-being? Fuck you. Hell, I've killed more gooks than most of your squads put together. My body counts make you look good, so as far as I care, you can kiss my ass."

I got up and walked out.

Evidently they didn't take it well, because that afternoon three soldiers with guns came and arrested me. I was put on a chopper to DaNang, then Stateside with orders for a mental evaluation. They took my rifle.

At Camp Pendleton the psycho docs started to work on me, insisting I stay in the hospital, "to re-adjust," they said. Old habits were hard to break. It was a month before I could sleep more than an hour at the time, wouldn't take a bath, and some nights used shoe polish to camo my face and roam the halls. After a few weeks, I was escorted to the head of the Psychiatry Department. A Navy Captain was reading my file. When he looked up, I could see concern in his face. "Is there any particular reason you sleep underneath your bed?"

"Just more comfortable." I stared at him, over him, around him, and moved my chair so I could see the door, not wanting my back exposed.

He watched me, then looked down at the papers. "Says here your commanding officer thinks you have lost touch with reality. Do you think you've lost touch, Sgt. Jacobs? Given what you've been through, it's perfectly understandable."

"Never thought about it like that." I sat perfectly still, like something wild waiting to pounce if given the chance. I could tell he was uncomfortable, squirming, sensing the danger in the room with him.

The Captain eyed the door and I knew he was considering his chances if I went berserk. "Spend some time thinking about it. In the meantime, we can't have you up wandering around all over the place at night. You're scaring the shit out of the nurses and staff when you just suddenly appear." He leaned back. "We can put you in a locked ward if you would feel more comfortable, if it would alleviate some of your fears."

I never moved or blinked, knowing I could go over the desk and kill the bastard before anyone could save him. He leaned toward me. "You're not in the war zone any more, Sgt. Jacobs. There is nothing to be afraid of here. No one is going to hurt you. We're trying to help you, but you need to help yourself as well."

"If you want to help me, send me the fuck back. I'll find my own way home when the war is over." I lit up a smoke and blew it in his face.

"You know there's no way that's going to happen." He looked at me with impatience, the tone of his voice scolding. Both of us knew he wasn't nothing but a lap-licking piece of Sailor shit who couldn't make it as a Marine

They gave me pills and I began to sleep longer. Nightmares came regularly, faces frozen in death, just like Snake warned me. It was like my brain was doing a replay of each kill. In my dreams, I could see every expression, smell every smell, and relish the sweet taste in my mouth. It became hard to know if I was awake or asleep, so I would lie still under my cot until something told me which it was. The docs kept giving me different stuff, trying to help me distinguish what was real from imagined, but I knew I wasn't getting any better; drugs would never cure what I had.

Convinced I would never get out unless something changed, I finally quit taking the medicines, started telling them what they wanted to hear, and lying on my bed pretending to be asleep. I even began to shower every day and agree with all their bullshit babble. After six months, they thought I was under control and assigned me to a training outfit in the sniper school. I hated it.

It seemed some days my sky would start to clear, and slowly I did begin to remember. Flashes of my life would show up unexpected when I smelled a certain scent or heard a person say something that triggered a memory. Ray Jacobs was starting to reappear.

Regular duty didn't do it for me anymore. Having to deal with other people only increased my frustrations. Most of them had heard stories of what I did in Vietnam and knew the name Ghost. I tried to help train the young warriors, envying their future, but wasn't any good at it. How do you teach a man to become invisible? I saw my face in theirs, knowing what was coming for them, and repeated Snake's warning about the road they were fixing to take. Just like I had, they all ignored it.

Alcohol became the best medicine for me, starting with a pint a day, then working up to a fifth. Pretty soon I was carrying a forty-five, slipping around at all hours of the night, occasionally being dragged in by MPs to sleep off a binge. Finally, the Marine Corps had had enough, sent me to Camp Lejeune in North Carolina, gave me a medical discharge, and took me to the bus station. They never even said thank you.

At my old home the house was empty, and looked like it had been for a while. So, I roamed from place to place the next twenty years, wandering around on the tips, living under overpasses, and sleeping on cardboard, longing for the freedom of the bush. One day I decided to hitchhike to the Great Smoky Mountains, pitched a tent deep in the woods, and survived the best way I could, sometimes doing work for local farmers in trade for food or rotgut moonshine.

My nickname got a revival when I would walk out of the fog of an early morning, on top of a man before he ever heard me. If you're out camping high in the mountains of North Carolina, you might hear tall tales of the Ghost of the Appalachians. If you find peanut hulls around your fire, and you feel that slight rise of the hair on your neck like you're being watched, you just might be right.

Sleep well.

Peace Be Upon You

Michael Lythgoe

Sometimes the Tailor hears bees
above his antique sewing machine.
He works in North Waziristan.
His designs are simple, cheap, reliable.

God willing

He starts with a sturdy cotton vest.
Surplus military gear from the local bazaar.
Thick straps secure it against the torso.
Add fabric pouches. Stuff with acetone
peroxide powder popular in Pakistan's
tribal regions. But today he kneads
doughy plastique, C4. Flattens the sticks
and packs them in thirteen pouches sewn
on the outside of the vest.

He slathers on glue with a brush. Tailor
works like a painter. Impasto. Thick.
Artistic design: shrapnel placed one nail,
one piece of jagged metal at a time.
Pressed in with patient precision.
He puts on marble-sized ball bearings;
he sticks in the nails. Finally, he
adds shiny twisted childrens' jacks.
A blasting cap is last, stuck in the C4 putty,
attached by wires to a nine-volt battery.

A cheap detonator switch is sewn
into a pocket that zips shut to slow down
the excitable martyr.

Peace be upon you

The Jordanian pediatrician
stars in a video and meets an Afghan
driver on the border
beneath wide orbits of a robot plane.

The doctor sees the large airfield
as he rides closer, and is cleared in the compound.
He phones a secret agent standing with an American.

You will treat me like a friend, right?

No pat down. No searches. At Khost,
the Subaru stops in front of a group of men and women.
The doctor steps from the car and disappears

in a flash of brightness.

God willing

Peace be upon you

KINGS OF FIRE AND WATER
~ Fred McGavran ~

"Who's he?" Ensign Scintilton said as he and the boat officer ducked into the cooking tent.

Dressed in a T-shirt, gray shorts, and sandals, the old man was standing beside a large pot with the self-conscious smile of someone who didn't know the speaker's language, or didn't want to betray that he did. Both Scintilton, early twenties, about six feet tall, thick glasses, black hair, dark green fatigues, and the boat officer, sandy haired, similarly dressed, and hardened by ten months in country, towered over the old man.

"His boat was tied up along the canal when we got here," said Lieutenant (junior grade) Nelson.

Grunting, the old man broke open a case of frozen rabbits and held one over the pot with the delighted grin of an obstetrician holding up a new baby. The American officers shifted and looked away.

"Maybe you should be careful, Frank," Scintilton said. "I've heard of them hanging around a camp pacing it off for a mortar attack."

"See that turban? I don't think he's Vietnamese. Maybe Cambodian."

With a little cry, the old man dropped the frozen rabbit into the cauldron. The two officers left the tent. Like an animated machine, the old man was breaking rabbits out of the ice and dropping them into the pot.

Finding it as stifling in the late afternoon sun as in the tent, Scintilton and Nelson watched the steam drift into the other tents, where the crews for the night patrols were getting up from sweat-drenched cots.

"Why would the Navy buy frozen rabbits by the case and ship them to the Mekong Delta?" Scintilton wondered.

"One of the sailors asked him what he wanted to fix for supper, and he said, 'Lappin,'" Nelson said. "Lappin's a great name for a cook, don't you think?"

"*Le lapin* is French for rabbit," the supply officer said.

"He must think you're the answer to a prayer."

Harris Scintilton had come up to the camp near the Cambodian border with the relief boats carrying fresh provisions from their base barge at Tan An. The boats were drawn up along the canal: six PBRs, fiberglass patrol boats bristling with machine guns; two Tango boats, armored river boats with a twenty millimeter mount on the bow; and a large armored monitor, the command boat, a shoebox-like craft with the only air conditioning and flush toilet in miles. A sailor with an M-16 was waving at a sampan across the canal.

"I've got to talk with the Lieutenant about tonight's patrol, Harris."

"I'll go back to the tent," the supply officer said. "There are some things I should check."

Across the canal, the man in the sampan seemed to be stretching to see something through the boats.

"*Dee dee mau!*" cried the sailor, telling the man to go away in Vietnamese and raising the automatic rifle.

The turbaned head ducked, and the boat darted away like a startled insect on a pond.

A quarter of a mile beyond the tents was a Vietnamese Army compound surrounded by a mud wall.

The Romans built forts like that, Scintilton thought. Or the Celts, after the legions withdrew.

A little farther down the canal was an Army firebase where they had flown in long-range artillery for the operation. Harris was wondering how long the mud walls would stand after the Americans withdrew, when he realized he was standing beside the cook again. The old man raised a stone crock and poured a clear liquid into the cauldron. Scintilton smelled the savory odor of fermented fish.

"*Nuoc mam?*" he named the favorite condiment of the Vietnamese.

"*La sauce*," the old man corrected him. "*Ici on parle Francais.*"

"What're we having tonight, Lappin'?" one of the sailors asked, bending over the pot. "Whew!"

"*Le lapin!*"

"Know what that means, Sir?"

"It means rabbit."

"Sure don't smell like rabbit to me," the sailor said, pulling out a pack of cigarettes. "Here, Lappin'. You want one?"

With an expression of genuine pleasure, the old man accepted a filter tip and let the sailor light it.

"He lives for cigarettes," the sailor said.

The old man inhaled like a connoisseur savoring the nose of his wine. Suddenly he bent double, coughing convulsively. When he finally looked up, Scintilton thought he saw red spittle on his lips.

"*Pardon,*" the old man whispered.

"Those things can be killers," the sailor said.

The old man wasn't listening. He was looking out the tent flaps toward the canal where the sampan had just slipped back into view.

"Didn't taste like rabbit to me," said the sailor.

"More like something in a Chinese restaurant," the radioman agreed.

Supper was finished, and the night patrol crews were savoring the last minutes before going down to the boats. Scintilton and Nelson carried their trays back to the cooking tent where the old man had started washing. Other men followed.

"Ask him where he learned to cook, Harris," Nelson said.

Scintilton was startled by the answer.

"What did he say, sir?" asked the sailor, who had come up behind them.

"He said he learned on the ship to France, before they made him king."

"King of what?" laughed the sailor. "All he has is a bed roll."

He kicked a bundle of rags by one of the tent posts.

The old man spoke sharply.

"He says not to touch it," Scintilton said.

Laughing, the sailor grabbed the rags.

"Well, will you look here."

Inside was a sheathed sword with a jeweled pommel and grip and curved blade.

"Let's see what you got here, Lappin'," he said, starting to draw it.

With a cry the old man leapt at him, snatching the sword away. Startled, the sailor moved toward him.

"Leave him alone," Scintilton ordered.

The sailor wavered between the old man and the officer.

"Why should I let some gook push me around?"

"He says if you draw the sword, the world will end in fire."

"Bullshit," said the sailor and stalked away toward the boats.

Scintilton and Nelson watched the old man wrap the sword in the rags again and then set it carefully by the post. On the road behind him soldiers were straggling out of the Vietnamese Army compound to take their positions for the night.

"It's time to get under way," Nelson said.

Scintilton kept looking. There was an American with the soldiers, probably an Army advisor. He carried his weapon like he thought he might have to use it.

There would have been a few Romans left, too, he thought, trying to hold the native troops in line when the barbarians started towards them across the fields.

"We better go, Harris," Nelson said.

The Vietnamese on the road were slowing, as if their energy was fading with the sunlight.

"'*Revoir*," Scintilton said to the old man, and followed Nelson down to the boats.

Two of the fiberglass patrol boats led the patrol, followed by a Tango boat with a 20-millimeter cannon. If they hit an ambush, the patrol boats would race through it, while the armored boat blasted back with its cannon. Putting on a flack jacket and a helmet, Scintilton felt his heart beating against the stiff cloth and sensed the fragility of his life here. Half a mile from their base they turned out of the canal into the river to Cambodia.

The engines deepened and their bow pointed toward the setting sun. Feeling the boat rise, the two officers gripped the canopy over the coxswain flat. Twenty yards astern came the second patrol boat, and behind it, running stiffly through the rolling water, was the Tango boat. Between the trees they glimpsed deserted fields. At a bend they startled two water buffalo drinking in the shallows and sent them lumbering back into the trees.

Who had driven them there? Scintilton wondered. And who would stroke their necks to calm them, saying the smell of the white man was like a passing dream?

The radio crackled, testing, assuring. It had been a long day for the supply officer, rising before five for the ride up river, then starting out on a night patrol. Suddenly exhausted, he sat down on the engine cover. A few feet away, Nelson was talking to the coxswain, while the stars were appearing one by one in the enveloping sky. There was a rich, green smell from the fields, as if farmers had just finished planting and were strolling home to rest. Eyes blurring, Harris concentrated on holding his rifle to keep from falling asleep.

"Harris," Nelson said.

Gripping his M-16, the supply officer stood up.

An orange glow had spread across the water. Over the canopy Scintilton saw the sailor who had taken the Cambodian's sword train his gun mount toward the light. Something was on fire, silhouetting the trees.

"Stand by," said Nelson.

Then they saw the burning hut. Like a charcoal lattice, the reed frame glowed in the blaze. Incredibly bright, the fire sparked and hissed in the jungle night.

"It's not burning," Nelson whispered. "It's on fire, but it's not burning."

Suddenly the Tango boat behind them erupted, slashing the night with orange shells.

"Test firing, sir," the coxswain said.

The tracers streaked through the hut but did not touch the burning frame. The boats went around a bend, and night settled over them again. Scintilton had just sat down on the engine cover when the bank exploded, slamming Nelson against the radio.

"Flank speed," shouted Nelson.

Scintilton was flat on the deck, breath sucked out of him.

"Delta Six," Nelson called into the radio as the boat leapt out of the water and spun toward the bank like a canoe caught in a whirlpool.

Water sluiced over the side, rolling Harris against the engine covers.

Gasping, he looked up at the trees just as the coxswain swung the boat away from the darkness. There was another explosion on the bank; he could smell its hot breath.

Somebody has to start shooting back, he thought wildly, groping for the M-16.

Behind them the boats spurted red, slicing the night with fire. Then their boat trembled; the gunners were shooting, screaming back at the crashing shadows. Nelson was yelling into the radio.

Who can save us? Harris thought, blindly firing at the trees.

Reaching for another clip, he glanced at the bow. Like a gray nightmare, two columns of water rose ahead of them. He nearly fell over the side as the coxswain banked right and then left around them.

"Cease fire! Cease fire!" Nelson called, shaking Scintilton's flack jacket. "Anybody hit?"

Suddenly the night was silent again; its terrors stilled like a madman strapped to a cot when the Haldol takes hold. No one answered. The machine gunners were jacking new belts into their weapons. Scintilton could hear the radio again. It was all right; no one had been hit.

"I called in an artillery strike," Nelson said. "We have to turn around. We're nearly in Cambodia."

Ahead of them something thudded into the earth.

"There they are," said Nelson. "Those are ours."

Scintilton could hardly breathe.

"You only have to worry when you hear them crack," Nelson said.

The boat officer spoke to his coxswain, and the boat slowed to turn.

My God, thought Scintilton. We're going back through there.

His fingers tightened on the M-16. He had been holding it like a talisman that could frighten away evil with its rattle. Then he remembered the old man's sword.

"You cover the starboard side, Harris. I'll take port," said Nelson. "Got enough clips? Good. Here we go."

As they turned the bank swung close and then started to move astern. Ten yards away they passed the second patrol boat. Like toys drawn on a string by a child, the column reversed course. Pitching, they crossed the Tango boat's wake. Nelson spoke into the radio again.

It's like fireworks when everything goes off at the end, the supply officer thought.

The boat was hardly moving as the last shells from the firebase dropped into the fields half a mile away. Then the engines deepened, the bow rose, and they were running for their lives down the river.

We're going to make it, Scintilton thought. The artillery silenced them. Thank God for the Army.

He saw the burning hut through the trees.

When we're by it, we'll be safe, he thought.

He felt the first explosion before he heard the rush of air. Like dreams shaken off in an uneasy sleep, the demons had returned. Rolling, gripping, leaping, they danced around the boats. Rattles did not scare them; talismans could not blind them. Naked, powerless, the boats would die on the water, burned by endless fire.

The hut's still burning, Scintilton thought.

The bow gunner saw it, too, and lashed the ash facade with red bullets. Spewing embers, the hut collapsed with a rush. The next explosion tore off Scintilton's helmet.

It won't stop until the world comes apart, he thought.

Still the water was flowing, and now there was deep blue over the trees. Scintilton knew they would make it when he saw the ashes on the canopy and realized it was morning.

It was as quiet returning to the canal as going out. They could see the trees near their camp clearly. Men were coming down to the bank to urinate. On the bow the gunner had his head down, sleeping through the last minutes of the patrol.

"Stand by," Nelson called to the gunner to tie up as they touched the bank.

The gunner didn't move.

"My God!" someone cried.

Scintilton climbed around the canopy onto the bow. The gunner had been decapitated. His black blood covered the deck.

"Frank," Harris called to the boat officer, then bent over the side and vomited.

Harris woke up just before the tent blew down. First dust swirled under the flaps, then the rotors hammered overhead, and then the tent posts leapt out, and the canvass collapsed over them.

"Oh!" he heard Nelson cry.

There was running and shouting outside, and in a few minutes they had peeled the canvas back. Scintilton climbed out from under his cot into the stifling morning. Twenty yards away a helicopter sat shuddering in the dust.

"Who's stupid enough to land a helicopter there?" Nelson began.

"It's the Admiral!" someone cried.

Scintilton shielded his eyes against the dust and sun. A short man in crisp fatigues and aviator sunglasses had climbed out of the helicopter and was striding toward a group of officers. With the smiling self-confidence of an officer who had never fought a battle, the Admiral exuded concern for his men and contempt for the enemy. Behind them the cooking tent had collapsed. Sailors with buckets were running up from the canal to douse the steaming canvas.

"He probably dropped by to inspire the troops," Nelson said.

The Admiral wasn't interested in inspiring the troops. His boats had been clobbered the night before, and he had lost a man. So he had come up himself to see why the Army's artillery couldn't silence a few gooks and to plan his counterattack.

"This is Lieutenant j.g. Nelson, my patrol leader," the Lieutenant said as Nelson and Scintilton approached. "And Ensign Scintilton, our supply officer. They had the night patrol."

"Well done," the Admiral said, pumping their hands. "Thanks to you, we have their positions pinpointed."

There was a crash under the cooking tent. Grunting, several men rolled back the canvass to expose the overturned cooking pot and the old man beside it. A strong, fishy odor enveloped the onlookers. Seeing Harris, the old man smiled and stood up with a Gallic shrug.

"Who's that?" demanded the Admiral.

No one answered. The boat officers looked at each other. Then Scintilton saw they were looking at him. After all, cooking was a supply function.

"Brought him aboard to help with the chow, sir," the supply officer said.

The Admiral wasn't listening to the Ensign.

"Get him out of here," he said to the Lieutenant.

The Lieutenant turned to the Ensign. Scintilton walked over to the old man.

"*Désolé*," he said softly.

As if sorry to have embarrassed a friend, the old man nodded and looked around for his bundle. When they had pulled the tent back, the rags had unwrapped, exposing the scabbard of his sword. He knelt quickly to cover it.

"Just a minute," said the Admiral. "What's that?"

In the dissonant syllables of his own language, the old man answered him.

"Let's have a look," said the Admiral, holding out his hand.

The squadron commander picked up the sword and handed it to the Admiral. The old man spoke again, this time in perfect French.

"He asks you not to draw it, sir," Scintilton interpreted.

"Why not?"

"He says if you draw it, the world will come to an end."

For a second the Admiral looked at the old man as if he believed him. Then he laughed. All the boat officers laughed with him except Nelson. Shaking his head in contempt, the Admiral gripped the hilt and drew the curved blade.

"See," he held it in front of the old man. "The world isn't going to end."

The Admiral in tailored fatigues and the Cambodian in shorts and turban were the same height. When the old man answered, Scintilton's stomach froze.

"Can you translate that?" the Admiral asked the Ensign, still smiling.

"'When the Lamb opened the seventh seal, there was silence in heaven for about half an hour.'"

As Harris spoke, the Admiral let the sword slide back into its sheath. The old man watched like a mandarin observing the humiliation of a coolie and spoke again.

"He said he's trying to compare it to something in our culture that you can understand," Scintilton translated.

"Here," said the Admiral, returning the sword. "Now tell him to go."

The old man received it like a tribute. Turning away, the Admiral led the boat officers down to the canal.

"Can you make sure he goes?" Nelson said.

"Let me get him some cigarettes."

The old man wrapped the cigarettes and a box of C-rations into his bundle. When Scintilton offered more, the Cambodian started to explain something and then had a coughing fit.

"It will not be long," he finally whispered.

Scintilton walked with him through the camp.

"Where are you going?"

They were speaking French.

"To the river. My people will find me there."

"I don't understand. Are you going home?"

"Stay with me awhile," the old man said.

Together they went up to the road and stepped around the concertina wire. The old man walked slowly, as if the bundle were very heavy. Artillerymen filling sandbags around the gun emplacements looked up as they passed.

"My only regret is that I never saw Paris," the Cambodian said. "Nice, Le Havre, Marseilles, but never enough time for Paris. If you left the ship for even a day, someone else would take your job."

"What happened?"

"When the Second World War came, my ship was interned in Saigon, and they made all of us leave. I walked back to Cambodia, past here." He laughed softly. "It took me four months. And when I arrived, they made me king."

"King of what?"

"King of fire."

"Why did you leave them?"

"The king of fire is not permitted to die like other men. As I grew old, I thought I was wiser than they. I thought I could escape my fate. I could no more escape than I could when I boarded the great ship to France. "

"Are they after you?" Harris asked.

"You saw them watching me from the canal," he said.

They had passed the firebase and were walking along the road away from the district town.

"Stop here," the old man said. "For you, it is not safe any farther."

There was a machine-gun emplacement beside the road. Scintilton saw Vietnamese soldiers watching them.

"You must be very careful," the old man said. "When the king of fire meets the king of water, they both must die, and all their followers with them. Go far away from here quickly."

"'*Revoir*," the American said, reaching for the old man's hand.

"'*Revoir, Monsieur* Scintilton."

The supply officer wondered how far the old man would get before his death caught up with him.

The next day Nelson's boats were rotated downriver to the barge at Tan An, and Scintilton rode with him. It was a bright morning, and as they turned into the river from the canal, the supply officer felt like a student leaving school for the summer. The water was high, and they rushed down the river level with the empty fields. Sometimes they saw bunkers in the trees, but Nelson said not to worry as long as there weren't any firing slits facing the river. Until they reached the villages above the city, they only saw one other person. Arms tied at his sides, he was kneeling on the bank, frozen at the moment of death.

The gunners trained their weapons, and Nelson picked up the binoculars. After a second he handed them to Scintilton. The supply officer took off his glasses and focused on the shore. Harris had seen many bodies in Vietnam, some drifting bloated down the river, some sprawled and flayed by artillery in the fields. But he had never seen one propped up like the corpse of a guillotined king for the crowd to see. The turban had unrolled from the head, and the arms were black with blood. An eyeless face looked up at the sky. If the rags that had wrapped the sword had not been beside him, Scintilton would not have been sure it was the old man.

That night Scintilton was on the top deck of the barge, watching the Vietnamese howitzer in the emplacement beside the river fire illumination rounds. Long seconds after the gun banged, the flares would open to float over the empty fields outside the city like tapers for the dead.

"Harris?" called Nelson.

The wardroom movie was over, and the boat officer had come out on deck looking for his friend.

"Did you hear what happened on our patrol?"

The supply officer did not answer.

"It was the Army shelling us. Can you believe that? They have the river covered by radar, and whenever they see anything moving, they just shoot."

The parachute on the last flare had caught on fire and was spiraling to earth. Their own fire had killed the gunner.

"Remember the place where we saw the burning hut?" Nelson said. "It won't be there after tomorrow."

"What's happening?"

"The Admiral's putting in a B-52 strike."

"There isn't anyone there," Scintilton said.

"Keep it secret, Harris. They're pulling all the boats back to camp."

In the early afternoon, the supply officer was on the pontoon alongside the barge talking with the engineers about parts for a boat. It was so hot they would have welcomed rain, but the sky was clear, too clear for thunder. They stopped talking to listen. The sound was like a faraway motor, starting slowly, growing deeper, then rumbling. As suddenly as a lawn mower in summer, the sound stopped.

Scintilton spent the rest of the afternoon in the supply office. Just before closing, while the clerks were covering the office machines, the boats were called away. He went out on deck and saw Nelson running down the ladder to his boat with his flak jacket and helmet.

"What's happening?" Harris called.

Nelson stopped and looked up.

"They screwed up the B-52 strike."

"They bombed the wrong target?"

"They bombed our camp."

When the kings of fire and water meet, their worlds come to an end, Scintilton remembered.

Below on the pontoon, they were waving at Nelson to hurry. Scintilton watched the boats depart, the sky darken in the evening, and the flares leer out of their canopies. Late that night when he couldn't sleep, he opened the Bible to *Revelations* to be sure he had heard the old man correctly. "Then the angel took the censer and filled it with fire from the altar, and threw it on the earth; and there were peals of thunder, voices, flashes of lightning, and an earthquake."

The sword had been drawn and the prophecy fulfilled.

Jody Got my Girl and Gone
~ Monty Joynes ~

My soul is muddy, my tired feet trying to force an illusion from the physical act of walking. Every time your boot marks an oozing step in the clay-sand soil, you can close your eyes until you are afraid to stumble, and try to remember how she was in bed. It seems a good trick. To forget for unmeasured steps that you hurt all over, that the steel pot has creased your forehead, that you hear the distant remains of automatic fire and the artillery, mortars pounding their thudding rhythm that means you soon may bleed. What did your college friend poet say? "You don't know what you are about until you see yourself bleed." Think about him, about that line. Then concentrate on what she wore the last time you saw her. Anything, anything that will take you out of the now.

How long has it been? How many novels ago? How many war flicks ago did it take to put you here? Where did the adventure go? I don't remember dirt and smell as props in those scenes. At what moment did war start to mean sore feet, bad food, no sleep, and just filth? Stale sweat seems to defy glory. Glory is clean and shining; we are leper-dirty. I buried her letters in a cat hole, her holy letters, so that I could carry a few extra rounds.

My beard is thick and oil smooth from so much living. I breathe down my shirt, snort a breath to cool my chest and smell the pungent updraft. Sweet life smell despite the tendency to despise that class of odor. But in the now, we live on ourselves, in ourselves, under and by ourselves.

The one behind has seen me sniff myself, has exaggerated the act with raised arm and said with mocked enthusiasm. "Damn, we stink good!"

Yes, we smell alive, and that is a different odor from the one of death. Have you ever been conscious of the human dead? Death is a corruption of will that makes nature rebel against that which it created. It covers its shame with rapid decay, and the once life-object spews out the breath of hell. Hot, moist, and confined it is, grasping the molecules of the air and squeezing them into submission. And that thing-pungent-ghost penetrates to cause a chemical reaction within the senses of the living. That reaction is fear.

Bottle it. Put it in an aerosol can. Spray it in the face of Congress, in the faces of the profit-makers. Watch their pusillanimous rage. When we start sending politicians to the front, there will be fewer wars.

I ache in every joint. My senses are overexposed to the point of pain. My complaint is wasted on men in the same condition. I am learning to understand hate. You hate death so much until you hate life. And when you hate life, you become a hero.

We pushed through a piece of landscape today. We pushed, erupting its soil, firing its vegetation, scarring it with our arms and our army. The day was fast. We marched into position and then ran, and fell, and followed a tank. I killed some men, I think. Mud-close to this foreign earth, my barrel was hot, hotter than a runner's breath. I held my panting in swallows to get sight-picture after sight-picture and squeezed off rounds I forgot to count until the magazine was empty, the bolt locked open, and I was suddenly afraid when I squeezed, and there was no recoil. Reload. Scream for ammo. Fire at silhouettes who rushed and fell and died concealed from my seeing. They jumped up in threes and tens, a sight-picture of four seconds. I fired and they fell. But were they merely diving for cover? Was it a coincidence that my shot and their falling happened so close in time?

Oh, we took some ground today. A field between two hills. We march now and at dark I will fix bayonet. The click tells me that I am brave. I can pause then to eat a can of stringy beef and a few hard crackers among bodies I might have killed. Old dead. New dead. I never feared a jam in my weapon until I stopped running.

This mud is sandpaper through my fingers. There are a few round, cool pebbles you suddenly want to put into your mouth. You can pretend that the artillery is a July fireworks display and that the distant pounding emanates from parade drums. You think, you close your eyes to dream, and you're able to shrink out of your helmet crease, out of the stone-block boots, the bandoleers that remind you that you are an instrument of firepower. Tonight you will lie on your side and watch the line of her pouting lips. You will make the burning stop in your eyes. You kiss the steel and it tears your lip to blood. Look quick into the night. Remember where you are but not why. Tomorrow is another day, and tonight you cannot rest.

I bleed. My blood is the red of flags and posters—on my hands, woven into the indentations of my fingers, dark on my clothing, suddenly becoming a wonderful hue when held against the late afternoon sun. I really don't know if I have been shot. My senses have been so full of targets that it was only during this march that I noticed blood dripping off the tips of my fingers. Little streams down my arm, red-wet, the creeping sting that turns into a bite and finally a gnaw. It throbs with warmth and I smile hot air out of my nostrils. I am not hurt; I am merely leaking life. It is just an inconvenience, another petty bother among the thousands exercising my modalities. I have stopped asking why or how. You endure and make a picture of what will be after all this. You live the dream of her and hide in it every time you are afraid to think. You lie to yourself until the real is the dream and the dream is true reality.

Her letters are gone. Even the one you tried to read by the glow of a cigarette under a poncho. The early ones that even smelled like her perfume, so excited, with runs in the ink from her real tears. She repeated the dream so many times and in so many ways that you almost accepted it as something that once had been. You could surprise her at school. Just appear as she turned a corner. That would be the end of circumstances, parents, time, and distance. She would drop her books, her purse. She would run on the street and cry in your arms. Neither of you would ever have to be alone again. Both of you would be the dream from the moment you saw each other.

Strong man—muscle strong, action strong, intellect strong—how can you corrupt this dirt and stench with the image of her? How can you mollify war with a soft caress? Rage is your safety. For rage is physical strength, and strength is survival, and survival from day to day is sweet human sweat, nothing more. Hate, then. Hate them who hate you and die because they are the other side. They are only silhouettes, human-like machines, dope-driven. They are devoid of emotion. The pain on their dead faces, their screams, are clever psychological gimmicks contrived by the enemy to cull your discipline to kill. Rage and hate bring strength to your flesh, blind you to the petty pains. Pressure bandage your arm. Let the blood dry in thin tentacles down to your hand. Hate your body for daring to hinder you. Hate them. And finally hate her.

I keep walking. The concept of marching seems unrelated to what we are doing now. Stumble along together in the shock of ordered chaos. Victory is a word that can be used only by the observer. I will never speak it again. Taking a farm field, a life for every foot, is no glory for the men who lived it, not today, not in the now.

The two ragged columns wind down a narrow road. I remember a tank trail at Fort Gordon. Tall-standing young soldiers, uniform proud. . . . My God, I am still alive. Remember why I buried her letters. Remember to make rationalizations for the last one. My eyes cannot cry. Perhaps tonight when I forget to remember.

Now straighten up with a secret strength. Take a full thirty-inch step and sing the cadence you had almost forgotten: "It ain't no use in going home. Jody got my girl and gone."

Dissolution

Laurence W. Thomas

I loved that man.
Through the mud and sweat,
the hardening of bodies and honing of skills,
learning neither to think nor question,
we were trained in the futility of war.

And then we were in it.
Through sand and incessant sun,
the constant threat of mines and suicide bombers,
learning neither patriotism nor victory,
but that the will to live leads to hostility.

We became a team.
Covering each other's asses
as we burst into homes, blasting the nameless,
mindless of factions and principles,
we sang the song of termination.

We loved each other.
With the manly love of trust
and mutual dependence to save our skins
we loved, until one explosion
burst love into dissolution.

A Grunt Christmas
~ Larry Dishon ~

"C-Squad" second platoon was humping point for the company. The lazy fuckers were wading right down the middle of a shallow stream. The rest of the company was broken into mingled squads, alternating to the left and right of the water and busting their own trails trying to keep their feet dry. The unmistakable sound of rain on the top of the canopy stopped Captain Dryer in his tracks. In a hushed voice he told me to hold the company in place. Jojo was jerking me around as he struggled to free my poncho from my pack. I keyed the radio handset and just whispered, "Hold up," and waited as the four replies whispered back, "Copy." I didn't stuff the handset into my shirt just yet 'cause I knew Kevin would need to know why. When he asked I just whispered back, "Daddy has to pee! Shut up!"

No one was in a rush to poncho-up; this damn jungle was so thick it'd be ten minutes before we felt the first drops. Funny thing about stifling heat, high humidity, and a poncho, it creates a kinda chimney effect. Body heat collects and rises. BO and jungle rot drafts right up inside the hood. God help you if you fart.

Captain Dryer took the handset from my shirt. I eavesdropped long enough to find out we were gonna scout a defendable position for the night. He handed me back the radio and said "Give 'm five more minutes and let's get started."

Jojo shared a sticky lemon drop hard candy with me and we both leaned back on the same tree. I cussed the rain and fumbled for a cigarette. Before I could light up, the first drops were slapping the leaves above our heads, so I just stuffed the pack inside my helmet, keyed the mike, and said, "Saddle up."

Three, maybe four minutes later, brush rustling telegraphed the movement of the column. The rain was coming down steady so I stretched an arm over my shoulder to turn up the volume. I got maybe twenty clumsy steps down the broken trail when I heard squelch.

"Tell daddy we smell smoke."

"Copy that. Talk to me!"

All hell broke loose from the lead platoon and everybody but me and the captain hit the brush. My asshole puckered. I knew the drill. Captain took the radio and we went boot-deep into the stream. He was towing me along by the handset cord. He loved being shot at! We passed about twenty troops, all prone in the brush, burning up ammo, shooting at ghosts. I heard a few barks of AK and the zing and buzz of free-agent lead pass overhead. Captain Dryer abandoned me and charged ahead screaming, "Hold your fire! Hold your fire!"

I ducked behind the biggest tree I could find just as I heard that dreaded scream for a "Medic!" echo through the jungle.

The sixty got quiet and one by one the M16s settled down. I was asking C platoon Radio Telephone Operator for his status on the radio, but no answer. Finally an unfamiliar voice said, "Two wounded, two dead. We need medivac!"

Medivac was inbound, eight minutes out. I relayed the news to Captain Dryer. My shaky voice gave away my scared-shitless reaction to seeing C platoon's RTO laying face up, staring into the rain. Doc Adis pulled the poncho over his face and went back to the wounded. Another contorted body lay face-down to my left. The sergeant stripes on his shirt confirmed who it was, no need to look. The medivac pilot's voice crackled through the static on the radio, updating his Estimated Time of Arrival, but I couldn't catch it. I made my way to Doc for his assessment of the wounded. The rain, the poncho, the confusion, and the fuckin' jungle made every step a test. Doc, as usual, had both wounds dressed and was already prepping them for the chopper. The pilot crackled in my left ear again just as the report from our recon squad was droning in my right. I handed Captain Dryer the recon squad and answered the pilot.

He was asking me to mark my location so I called out "Smoke!" as loud as I could and tossed a can into the clear. The smoke canister popped and sputtered out a plume of red that rolled across the jungle floor. I yelled into the mike, "Smokes away!" as the slapping blades of the chopper came and went above the canopy some distance away. The chopper made two more passes before the smoke had climbed above the canopy downstream.

The next transmission wasn't good. "No fuckin' way red smoke! I can't even cable down in this weather! You're under triple canopy at least! I'll look for an opening."

Doc was listening with me and said, "Forget it for now. We'll manage."

I told the pilot we were gonna punt, but he made two more low passes before his whop-whop-whop faded into the incessant drone of raindrops cascading down from a hundred feet or more up, leaf to leaf.

The jungle rained steady now and would for the next four days. The stream swelled quickly behind us, so we had to claw our way up out of the valley. Misery set in two hours up the slope. By day three we broke into a burnt-out clearing near the ridgeline where limbless, burnt-tree carcasses circled a crater lake.

Home sweet home.

We circled the lake, too, and stretched our ponchos collectively in groups between the charred remains. Food was scarce by day four and we were drinking rain water collected off our ponchos and tainted with iodine. No one talked anymore except for Doc and the wounded guys. The steady patter of the rain on the ponchos and splats on the saturated ground had long since stolen sanity from circumstance.

The marshmallow cloud that had wallowed around in the valley below us for days dissipated into a mist that capped our make-shift POW camp. At times I could see other zombies across the pond huddled over the blue blaze of a C-4 fire. The mist lingered most of the day but the rain stopped. A silence settled over the camp like a warm blanket on a rescued victim. We all listened in unison.

By two that afternoon there were voices muttering from every direction around the pond. Half-naked bodies wrung the misery from their clothes and hung them to dry. Complaints of empty stomachs and piss that was red from iodine grew into a discourse that prompted Captain Dryer to huddle with his cadre.

I was already on the radio with battalion supply, begging for priority and listing item by item quantity in order of urgency. A small group of the platoon RTOs had gathered with their lists prompting me with hand gestures and primal grunts to punctuate their lobbied-for positions. My proper radio protocol sank to begging and pleading until the bargain was struck. We'd get ammo before dark but everything else would have to wait for first light.

Word spread from camp to camp in minutes and free-trade bartering commenced. A dry cigarette would buy almost anything. I had four left, high and dry, tucked away in the top of my helmet. Jojo slopped through the mud grinning ear to ear and dancing two ration cans like hand puppets right up to my face. Sliced peaches and beef in succulent broth topped the menu in complement to my contribution of pork and beans and a can of pears. We ate in celebration and with unspoken hesitation, praying the weather would hold and this wouldn't be our last meal.

Eight crates of ammo, one bundle of C-4 with a coil of detcord and medical stuff arrived at dusk. The chopper had to hover while the door gunner heaved the wooden crates out into the mud. Everyone was cussing the prop wash as it furled ponchos round the trees and lifted the sodden earth into a blinding-brown shit-cloud. The sun set to softer and softer murmurs and the click-click-click of magazines being refilled.

The night was way too short and the sun, which we called Sol, was back in full intensity. Complaining was the order of the day. I made my status report to battalion and waited for the encrypted call back about resupply. My last instant coffee and last cigarette left me a little dizzy, so I spent my time cleaning the crud off my rifle and watching others take baths and do laundry around the lake. Two squads were sent back to the valley to retrieve the casualties. A swarm of volunteers rigged explosives to the stand of tree stubs right where the ridge crested.

"Fire in the hole!"

Eight explosions later, we had a make-shift landing zone.

Resupply would take all day since only one chopper was available and it would have to make shuttle trips. Jet turbine whine from the valley brought everybody to their feet. We all stood and stared as

Medivac skimmed over the treetops below us and rose with thunderous chops up the ridge. It settled onto our LZ and rolled the yellow smoke into a huge doughnut shape as the wounded were lifted aboard and two body bags were unloaded. The yellow smoke cloud turned to shitty brown as we cheered and waved to the two morphine patients and chopper crew.

Rations and the first blivet of water were next on the pad. Third platoon hustled the cases into stacks and stood guard against interlopers until all stacks were equal. An early lunch seemed in order and distribution went without a hitch.

As my LARP (Long-Range Reconnaissance Patrol Rations) water was coming to a boil, the radio squawked. Heavy, muffled breathing, like that of some pervert from a bad movie, licked the inside of my ear. A voice talking behind a stuffed-up nose said, "We're just outside the tree line. Make sure those fuckers know it's us!"

"Copy, rescue. Permission to enter."

I stood tall and blared across the compound, "HOLD FIRE! RESCUE IS INBOUND!"

Captain Dryer straightened his uniform, shouldered his weapon and wove his way through the maze of makeshift tents to wait for our losses. Twelve exhausted soldiers emerged from the jungle. The fourth and seventh man in the column each struggled proudly, shouldering the weight of poncho-draped corpses. Several troops rushed out to help with the burden.

The company collected into a mass around the chopper pad where the two slick, black body bags lay waiting their ride home. A hatless Captain rested his rifle barrel on the toe of his boot and eulogized.

Midway through the sermon came the call from the last of the resupply sorties. Captain Dryer never wavered as two ponchos and a dozen volunteers covered the body bags and held fast till the chopper rocked to a shaky landing. Both door gunners swung free and stood tall and rigid until Captain Dryer reset his hat.

Three large mailbags, sundries, and a final water blivet were exchanged for the two bags. Some saluted, some stood hand-over-heart until the chopper lifted and rolled down off the summit.

A sober mass ambled away from the LZ. Captain Dryer and the mail made the trek back to the command post. Today, First Sergeant

Griggs did the honor of sorting and calling the mail. He tucked a couple of letters inside his shirt; several others he stacked to the side without even looking up. We all knew. Even as the platoons came and went to gather the mail, there was little of the normal joy that mail normally raised.

I got four letters and two boxes which I arranged by postmarked date. Past experience dictated that the boxes should be the first opened. All sorts of gifts from the world waited. I opened the larger of the two first to find it held a miniature Christmas tree. It certainly was late December but thoughts of Christmas lay buried beneath the day-to-day struggle of this safari. But that tree resurrected the true season. Suddenly it was Christmas! I stepped outside the poncho tent and held the tree to the sky and proclaimed, "MERRY CHRISTMAS!" Like the gophers in *National Geographic*, heads popped up all around. Cheers and joyful voices returned Merry Christmas as they recognized the evergreen symbol. Jojo helped me tie the tree to the tallest standing trunk outside our tent and the radio came to life with curious questions of what else had come in the packages.

Captain Dryer stood for the longest time and just stared at the Christmas tree. He and I exchanged a rare smile when he finally looked back. Not a word, just the smile.

The rest of the hot afternoon passed with relative calm. We read the letters over and over and shared the news from back in the world. I took my turn at guard duty and snacked on cookies from home, made canteen Kool-Aid, and fought off the homesickness that always came with the mail.

Once dinner was over the ritual that came with dusk began. Everything had to be readied for whatever surprises "Charlie" and "Night" might be planning. As the ponchos came down and the sun got ever closer to the horizon, that little tree perched overhead cast the longest shadow in the jungle. Lying on my back, with only the Christmas tree in view was transporting. I stared up through tears to say thank you for the Christmas cheer and silently said all the things that I couldn't say aloud. I imagined the words being carried into the cosmos and somehow you'd hear, "Thank you, I love you!" and know that all the miles between us, all the terrors that we both endured, could not break our connection.

Jojo had the last shift at monitoring the radio and woke me with his clumsy sorting through the ration cans for breakfast. I stood with my back to the morning sun and straightened the little tree. A slow gaze around the jagged circle of defensive placements brought a broad grin to my face and a dozen others. I mouthed "Merry Christmas!" between yawns and read the lips mouthing back.

The damn radio hissed and squawked. A monotone voice I knew all too well insisted on my attention. What followed was the typical one-sided directive. Mission first, scheduled departed time, coordinates for insertion. I dutifully asked for intel and any expectation of resistance. I got the usual need-to-know bullshit. Captain Dryer was shaving. He just grunted as I read off my notes. Without even missing a stroke, he waved the back of his hand at me and I spread the word.

Sorties of four choppers each came and went from our mountaintop LZ all morning. Circling like buzzards, one by one they swooped down and collected their loads. I hid under my poncho and yelled directions into the radio, avoiding the dust storm until their whining clatter faded into the valley. Between sorties, Jojo and I fumbled with the Christmas tree and argued about how best to pack it. Its sprawling limbs and delicate ornaments challenged our every attempt to wrangle it. We finally lashed it sideways atop the battalion radio. We'd run out of time and creativity. The last sortie was inbound and that was our ride back to the war.

I stood and faced the storm as the first three buzzards gobbled up all but the last five of us. Head down and leaning into the prop wash, I forced my overweight ass to jog and slide onto the floor of the last Huey. We had already lifted off the LZ when the door gunner slapped my shoulder and pointed to the Christmas tree spiraling down in exaggerated lazy circles, its ornaments ruffling like the skirt of a dancer. We couldn't help grinning as it danced. The hard right bank of our sleigh stole its finale from sight.

There it dances still, between heaven and earth.

AMPUTATED BONES AND VOMIT
~ Stanley Noah ~

During the First Battle of Bull Run, Stuart's new cavalry regiment was held in reserve, well behind the front lines. Between his unit and the battleground a school house had been converted into a field hospital. Doctors cut and sawed off legs and arms by the dozen, tossing them aside, until soon the area resembled a hog slaughter house. Eventually the number of body parts grew so large that the staff was forced to open two windows in the rear of the hospital and throw the limbs into large buckets located just outside. In the late afternoon Stuart was ordered to re-deploy his troops closer to the lines, and move up at a walk. The path took his troops behind the hospital where in formations of two the men got a long, slow view of the filled buckets of horror. Not yet engaged in battle, they were already being confronted by the remains of war. The sight and smell of decaying flesh in the heat of day caused the men to throw up, throw up over their pants legs, into their boots, and on to their horses. The conflict would last four more years and millions of screams. To the soldiers it would be four lifetimes.

The Last Cow

William Miller

My great-grandfather was
nine when the soldiers came.

Three of them crossed
the back field
with their rifles raised,
boots crushing the dry
stalks and sedge.

They asked his name,
then for water, why he
didn't drum like little
Rebs his age, march
at the front of the line.

He had a job, he told them,
a job here in the hills,
a home guard who took
care of pigs and mules,
widows and children
left behind.

Where were the slaves,
they asked,
the black bucks
all that blood was
spilled for, the flag
they kept shooting down?

His people didn't own
slaves, never had;
slaves belonged to rich men
who farmed bottom land
hundreds of miles
from here.
The soldiers walked past him
straight into the barn
as if they knew there was
at least one cow
to steal.

"Thanks, boy," they
said as they led her
away. "We're Sherman's
best. Got cities to burn!"

He watched them disappear
over the ridge, wondered
if he should tell someone,
everyone, that the war
was almost over,
the men were coming home.

But he didn't know
the day, the hour, and a
sick woman was waiting
for him to kill a chicken
in her dooryard,
mend her back fence.

He closed the stall behind him
and went out to fight
the war one more day,
fight while soldiers
drank milk for a sick baby.

Still Photograph: Lee's Funeral
William Miller

The old soldiers
and the still young
have filed from the church
where they said goodbye
to the man they followed
down a thousand bloody hills,
across fields of dead horses,
dying men.

They linger on the lawn
in dress greys pressed for
this terrible day, the smallest
brass button polished
brightly, their hats
in hand to show
even a private's sorrow,
the deepest respect.

Stories are told
in detail, how he never
drank or cursed even
when the day was clearly
lost, had to be forced
back from the range
of sniper fire, shells
exploding nearly at his feet.

They linger on the lawn
tell their stories again,
but in the left corner
of the picture,
a black boy sits on
the top of a fence,
his face turned away
from the soldiers and the church.

WAR MEMORIES
~ Henry F. Tonn ~
from the verbal history of Richard Daughtry

I never wanted to be a soldier. I wanted to be a football player. After playing halfback in high school, I went off to the University of North Carolina in 1938 with the intention of becoming a college star. But the coaching staff didn't see it that way. Instead of letting me run the ball, they had me blocking for other players in the backfield. I ended up carrying the ball once the entire season and finally left in disgust. My sophomore year I didn't play football at all and eventually dropped out of college altogether because I had no backup plan to being a football player. While I was contemplating my next move, the war broke out and I became a soldier just like everybody else.

In July of 1942, I went to Florida for a little boot camp and then to South Dakota where they taught me Morse code and how to shoot a machine gun. Unfortunately, they never issued me a machine gun, eliminating any chance of my demonstrating my skill in military combat. Next they shipped me to Wisconsin where I learned radio operation for a fighter plane. I specialized in the P-47. In July of 1943, I boarded the Queen Elizabeth for a five-day trip across the Atlantic to the British Isles. I was seasick the whole time. It was terrible. The ship went up and down, up and down. God, it makes me queasy to think about it even today. By the time our ship reached Scotland, I was so weak I could barely carry my bags down the gangplank. And I remember when my feet finally hit the ground a little boy approached me and said, "I'll take you to my sister for a cigarette." His timing was terrible: I wasn't in any kind of shape to take up his offer.

They transferred us by train to Colchester, near the east coast of England, where a covey of Air Force bases were located, and that's where I remained for the next year. P-47s accompanied bombers to Germany and I worked on their radios. When I wasn't working, I read or played cards or just shot the breeze. A lot of poker and blackjack was going on, but you had to be careful because some of those guys were professionals and would cheat the pants off you. They don't divulge that sort of thing in the literature about the war but that's the way it was: the American army was full of vultures. I don't remember any chess or checkers being played, but out of the whole squadron of 250 men, four of us played bridge, and we'd get together from time to time. And softball was popular during the summer.

I took the railway to London a couple of times on leave and wandered around the town to see the sights. We'd be accosted by prostitutes as soon as we emerged from the train. They were everywhere, offering you everything. We'd been thoroughly briefed on the diseases they could pass on, but plenty of guys succumbed anyway.

A joke that went around goes: A guy gets off the train in London and a prostitute approaches him and says, "I'll bet I can give you something you've never had before." And the guy shrugs and says, "The only thing left is leprosy."

I'm telling you, there is nobody hornier than an American soldier. The British were right: "They're oversexed, overfed, and over here." We were young, our hormones were raging, and there was no one to take care of our needs except prostitutes. It put you into a helluva fix. And as I look back on it, the horniest of the hornies were the American Italians. Being from the South, I'd met very few Italians till I went into the Air Force, but they certainly get my award for being the most willing to access all available opportunities. There were two guys from Providence, Rhode Island, who, well, if a mare galloped through our base, we feared for its virtue.

I met more girls from the general population in France than in England. They were always hanging around the American soldiers because we had cigarettes and chocolate, and sometimes that could lead to some promising relationships. You were always hoping to get lucky, of course, but often if things got too heated the French girls would say, *"Je suis bon,"* and you were out of luck. *"Je suis bon"* meant "I am good," which meant I don't sleep with American soldiers, or perhaps anybody else for that matter. I heard *je suis bon* entirely too often while I was in France. I understand the French are supposed to be more liberal about matters of the flesh than people of most nations, which is great. But I think I met every virgin in the country while I passed through. I was forced to be a lot more *bon* than I ever wanted to, I can tell you that.

I arrived in France several weeks after D-Day in June of 1944 where an air base had been set up to support the infantry. We got bombed and strafed periodically by the Germans, but, in general, we were pretty well protected by anti-aircraft guns on the perimeter. It didn't get too bad from my perspective till November arrived and winter started setting in. Europe had one of its coldest winters ever in 1945. In January and February the temperature rarely rose above freezing, and the nights were brutal. I slept in a tent with no heat. To keep yourself from freezing to death, you rolled yourself fully clothed in your flight jacket into your sleeping bag on your bunk and then covered yourself with whatever blankets you could find.

Sometimes I'd be up at five-thirty in the morning to get the planes ready. Snow covered the ground and we'd have to bulldoze it off before the planes could take off. I was a tech sergeant in charge of thirty-five planes and there was no option to rising early in the morning. At one point I didn't bathe for a month, just lived in my flight jacket. I had it rough, but I swear to God my hat's off to the infantry in our army who often had to live out in the open under those conditions. I don't know how they did it. It's a wonder every damn one of them didn't get Post Traumatic Stress Disorder.

Another thing I want to talk about is the food: it was terrible. In the morning we were served Shit-on-a-Shingle, which was some sort of chipped beef covered with white gravy on toast. It tasted awful to start with and by the time you got it to your tent, it was also cold. Lunch and supper weren't much better. I took to scavenging through the countryside when I was in France bartering with the farmers for eggs and apple cider. I'd give them a carton of cigarettes and they'd give me a couple dozen eggs and two pints of cider. Any time I could avoid eating service chow, I did. I've never understood why the food for American troops was so bad. I've read that the Italians ate spaghetti and the Germans ate sausages and the French ate, well, French food. Meanwhile, we ate crap. I read once that a group of German prisoners was complaining about the food, saying the Geneva Convention specifically stated that they should have the same food as the regular army. They were told this WAS what the regular army ate. They said, "*Mein Gott*, how do you live?"

We should do better.

Another thing I want to talk about is the swearing. If you don't know how to swear when you go into the service, you'll learn quickly. American servicemen swear about everything all the time. I came to think motherfuckingsalt was one word—my mother had just been mispronouncing it all those years. Sometimes in one sentence you would use more swear words than regular nouns, verbs, and adjectives. The officers swore just like the enlisted men. We had *that* in common. It was the only way you could get anything done. If I said, "Clem, take that mop and clean out the latrine," the guy would give me a blank look. But if I said, "Clem, take this fucking mop and get your goddamn ass over to the motherfucking latrine and clean the sonofabitch," he'd smile and say "Yes, Sarge," and hop right to it.

The pilots in our squadron ate better than the ground crew and I never begrudged them that privilege. Every time they went up in those planes they were challenging death. It was kill or be killed, to use the old cliché. You soon learned that you could have a close friend one day and he'd be gone tomorrow. A lot of pilots died through stupid errors, though, errors that had nothing to do with the war. I had a good friend once who was a pilot and he was in the air one day horsing around with another pilot directly over the field. They were flying parallel to each other and did simultaneous barrel rolls. Unfortunately, they came out of their rolls too close together and collided. My friend's plane spiraled down and smashed directly into a farmer's barn and exploded into violent flames. I hope he died on impact because that's a terrible way to go. What a ridiculous waste of human life, and this sort of nonsense happened all the time.

As the war progressed, you just got used to people dying. Thirty-five planes would take off in the morning and only thirty-three would return. You'd suddenly discover that you didn't have a second baseman on the softball team anymore because Bernie was gone. What an inconvenience! It sounds calloused but that's the way it was. War changes people in more ways than you can imagine. It's a wonder anybody's normal when they get back.

Here's another example of the same thing: I used to get drunk with one of the pilots and then we'd go up in the training plane for a joy ride. We'd buzz the French farmers in their fields, sometimes diving so low we'd make them hit to the ground to avoid us. They'd come up shaking their fists and using dirty French words. We'd laugh. But one day while we were horsing around, we ran into problems. When we tried to switch to the reserve fuel tank, it didn't catch, and the engine died. We went into a tailspin and dropped a thousand feet until the pilot got the plane under control. It burst my eardrum. He turned back to me and said, "I can roll the plane over and we can just drop out and parachute down if you'd like."

Well, that idea scared me to death. "What's the alternative?" I asked.

"The alternative is I take it down on dead stick. Of course, you know, that's dangerous. We might crash."

"Can you do it drunk?"

"Hell, I'm sober now," he said.

So was I!

He radioed ahead and informed them of our plight and then started circling the field. Two fire engines and two ambulances drove out to the runway and lots of men from the squadron came out to watch the show. In case you're not aware, it's hard to land one of those heavy planes without an engine, and many a pilot has died trying. I gave us a 50-50 chance. But he landed it, and I'm alive today to tell the tale. That's the last time I went up with him, though, drunk or sober.

Crazy things happen in war. Once in the early morning while we were all lined up for breakfast, a German bomber flew directly over the field. He was all shot up and flying sideways like a mangy dog slinking down a sidewalk. The plane was so low we could see the flight crew's faces, but we couldn't do a damn thing about it. Here we were, an air force squadron with one hundred and five planes on the ground, but not a single one ready to take off. If I'd had my carbine I could've shot them right out of the sky, but none of us was armed. We cursed about it all day. It was humiliating. He might as well have given us the finger while he flew by.

The best pilot I ever saw was Francis Gabreski. He led all European pilots in the World War II theater with twenty-eight kills, and was simply in a class by himself. His fighter group was the famous 56th, which registered more kills in the war than any other group in the Eighth Air Force. Francis was always looking for interesting sorties and he was friends with our squadron leader, so when our fighters were heading off to a promising place, he'd join us. He was that way: he did whatever he pleased. That probably kept him from achieving a higher rank in the Air Force than he did because he didn't play by the rules. But it also resulted in a lot more Germans dying in combat.

When he sat in a cockpit, the airplane fit around him like a suit of clothes. He did things other pilots simply couldn't imitate, even though they tried. I used to work on his radio and I never saw a bullet hole in his plane. He just flew too well to get hit by enemy fire. Every time he scored a kill, he'd do a barrel roll coming in to the base. On one occasion he did two but didn't get credit for either one. There was no independent confirmation. I once asked him how many planes he really shot down in his career, and he estimated seventy-five. But he never talked about them. The Air Force said twenty-eight and that's what he accepted.

On July 20, 1944, on what was supposed to be his last mission, he flew too low over an enemy field while strafing and his propeller hit the ground and he crash-landed. They caught him five days later in the woods and he was interviewed by the famous German interrogator, Hanns Scharff, who said, "We've been expecting you for a long time." Scharff smiled and held up a military newspaper showing Gabreski's twenty-eighth kill. Francis—Gabby, they called him—was a prisoner of war for the next ten months, but in April he came strolling into the camp after being liberated by the Russian army. He had this big grin on his face.

They called Gabreski cocky and arrogant, but I always liked him. He was friendly to ground-crew people like myself. He was a good man.

Of all the death and dying I saw, the worst was the concentration camp at Buchenwald. I've talked about it in the past but, interestingly enough, I forgot to reveal the worst thing I saw that day. It was so horrible I repressed it for seventy years. But one day it just popped into my head.

In Buchenwald, the Germans had something called "the killing room." It was a room constructed beneath the ovens to prepare human bodies for incineration. The prisoners—usually dead—would be tossed down a chute from outside and then stacked up. If for some reason someone were still alive, he would be clubbed over the head with a mallet and killed. They then transferred the bodies into the main room where a series of meat hooks were arranged on the walls. One hook would be attached to the wall and two others would be facing outward. The body would be hung by the neck, just under the jaw, from the two hooks so that the shoulders would sag and the body became straight. This was necessary in order to slide the body properly into the ovens above. When the body had hung for an established length of time, it was transported by elevator upstairs to the ovens.

As I have said, I arrived in Buchenwald about twenty-four hours after it had been liberated and a Jewish prisoner took me and some of my buddies around the camp. Of everything I saw, this was the most chilling. The Germans had tried to clean the place up and take the hooks down before they left, but four hooks still remained in place and you could see remnants of blood on the floor and walls. Our Jewish guide said he had known about the place for a long time but he never ventured anywhere near it until liberation. He said a senior German officer assured him that some of the men were still alive when put on the hooks and the death was agonizing. I understand that room can be seen today at Buchenwald because it's been preserved as a memorial. They call it the "execution room" now, but our guide definitely called it the killing room when our group passed through.

It perplexes me to this day that normal German people who had wives and children and the equivalent of white picket fences around their houses could also indulge in this kind of heinous behavior. I just don't understand it.

After Buchenwald, the war with Germany came to a rapid conclusion. Since we were still fighting the Japanese, our squadron was sent to southern Germany to prepare for jungle warfare. But the Japanese surrendered before we were deployed overseas. I am grateful to Truman to this day for dropping that second atom bomb. If he hadn't, there would have been more bloodshed—more pointless bloodshed.

It took us five days to cross the Atlantic by ship at the beginning of the war, but it required two weeks to get back home. This ship was simply slower. I was sick the whole time and so was everybody else. God, it was awful. The vomit in all the bathrooms was two inches thick. As far as I know, nobody ever cleaned it. I was never happier in my life than when my feet finally hit American soil.

I took a train directly to my home in Goldsboro, North Carolina, and tried to get my life together. Soon after, I moved to Wilmington, on the coast, where I managed to find a job. After six months or so, though, I started having trouble with dizzy spells and digesting my food. I went to a doctor and he said this was a case of delayed battle fatigue—he saw it all the time. He gave me some pills and told me to go fishing because it would relax my nerves. I did, and the problem eventually went away. I haven't had it since.

I feel fine now.

Friday Night, FOB Cobra

Hugh Martin

1.

Smith, shirtless, curls forty-pound
dumbbells, veins burst

like worms over his biceps. The curls
are part of his plan for home:

a sex life.

2.

On burn detail, Ritchey stirs shit
with a metal rod,

asks Carter—standing back with a smoke—
Doesn't it make you hungry?

3.

In Tower Ten, Stevens discusses mutual funds,
interest rates. He says a young guy like me

might spend all his money on a bike, a truck,
a house. He's taking his wife

for a cruise, investing the rest,
and that's what you do with money.

4.

Jones' brother sent him a twelve-pack
of UltraSensitive LifeStyle

condoms. The box reads:
almost like wearing

nothing at all. He cuts it out,
tapes it to the front of his flak vest.

5.

When asked why his hands are so hairy,
Kenson says, with a cup of coffee in one of them

and a ball of wet Copenhagen
bulging beneath his lip, *I ain't a fuckin' girl.*

He sips four pots a day, changes the grinds
once a week. The coffee tastes of steam and heat.

6.

Kellerman's wife divorced him over e-mail.

7.

Ski boils water in a canteen cup, adds Ramen,
slices of expired Slim-Jims. He discusses

the meaty juices, how the heat pulls them
for flavor. He says this meal is sacred.

8.

Sergeant Thompson has been in so many fights,
there is no cartilage left in his nose.

In line for the phone, he shows us:
bending it like an ear

with one finger, flat against his cheek.

9.

On marriage, Perry says, *It ain't like that.
You think you just walk in the door,*

*and she hands you a beer,
gives you a blow job.*

It ain't like that, he says. *Just wait,
it ain't like that.*

10.

Sprinkling hot sauce over cold, boiled potatoes,
Dempson talks about reading the paper,

the names of the dead. All of us know
he's slept with ninety-seven women.

After we finish our food,
he tells us about one.

JAPANESE OCTOBER
~ Frank Holland ~

While the medic tended the cuts on the faces and hands of the three soldiers, the most seriously injured from the accident, an aged Japanese civilian, lay dying on the floor. No one was doing a thing to save him. They hadn't even placed his stretcher on the examination table. They left it next to the door as soon as they carried him in from the ambulance.

I had walked across camp to visit my friends at the squadron hospital. Originally assigned here, I was transferred to a different medical unit two weeks earlier. I stopped at the dispensary when I saw an ambulance outside. Only one medic was on duty, treating the three soldiers. He walked past the stretcher to get bandages and antiseptic.

He called to me at the door, "Hey, Ralph, you want to give me a hand here?"

"Sure," I said. I went to one medicine cabinet, then another. I used to store first-aid supplies on the bottom two shelves where I could reach them immediately. Now everything had been rearranged. I finally found peroxide on the top shelf in back. With a wad of cotton I began cleaning the cut forehead of one of the injured soldiers. Foam bubbled from his wound. Another GI sat on a wooden folding chair, his knees wide apart to prevent their being spotted by blood dripping from a gash across the bridge of his nose. The third soldier had only a few scratches on his face and a skinned hand.

The Japanese man on the stretcher was not moving at all. His left foot wore a black shoe indented between the big toe and the other toes, the way a mitten separates the thumb from the rest of the fingers. His other foot, bare, was covered with gray dust. His right knee was flexed to the side so that his ankles nearly crossed. Streaks of blood, dry now, had run off his face and around to the nape of his neck. They collected there and seeped into the brown stretcher canvas.

Attached to a different unit now, I had no right to make suggestions, but asked anyway, "Did you call the captain?"

The medic was sticking a bandage on the soldier's sweaty forehead, but the tape kept curling off. "He's on strike."

"Strike?"

"If it's not a life-or-death emergency, he says he's on strike until they send him a replacement. He's our only doctor now."

I looked down at the Japanese man. "Why don't we put the stretcher up on the table?"

"Forget him. Give me a hand with this other guy. And get me some gauzes for his nose."

I found some in the medicine cabinet and pressed a gauze sponge across the cut. "Keep pressing," I told the soldier. "Like this. And hold your head back."

I stopped alongside the stretcher. The ride must have been bumpy. Dried blood streaks ran all directions from the man's nose and mouth. They lined his eye sockets, the wrinkles across his forehead, even his ear passages. Where they radiated over his cheeks and down the chin and neck, the red streaks created a grotesque mask that parodied the rising sun on the Japanese flag.

I crouched next to him and tried to see through the slits of his eyelids. His eyes appeared dry, blurred with dust. His lips had been cut by the broken teeth that protruded through a thick, dark clot that had formed across his partly open mouth. Using a fresh wad of gauze, I poured peroxide over it and then touched the pad lightly to the man's face to clear away any stains that might be hiding cuts underneath. When I moved past him, it seemed his eyes flickered a moment, but that could have been my imagination. I wanted him to sense that someone was trying to help him.

The medic noticed. "I said leave him alone. He's done for."

"I just want to see if he . . . ."

"Well, he's not!"

"If we turn him face-down . . . ."

"You gonna help me here?"

I dropped the used gauze sponges in the wastebasket and returned to the soldier with the cut nose. I pinched above the nose bridge between his eye sockets to slow the bleeding.

We all heard at once a deep, croupy cough from the man on the stretcher, rumbling like a bad chest cold. Pink foam splashed from his mouth, carrying with it the plug of clotted blood that had blocked his breathing. His eyes winced shut as he continued coughing.

"See?" I said. "He *is* breathing. Let's turn him over so the blood doesn't run down his throat."

Captain Jackson walked in at that moment. He grunted at the stretcher. Turning to the GI with the bandaged forehead, he asked, "What happened?"

"It was dark," he said, "and foggy. He hit us with his cart. I didn't even see him till just before we hit."

"You driving a jeep?"

"Yeah." The soldier eyed Jackson's gold bars. "Yes, sir."

The fellow with the bleeding nose said, "It didn't have any lights on it, sir. It was the Jap's fault."

"And it was too late to stop," the driver added.

Captain Jackson walked back to the stretcher and looked down. "No, he won't last long."

"Didn't I just say that?" the medic told me, loud enough for the captain to hear.

The captain examined the soldier's bleeding nose. He moved the wound right and left to see how deep it went. Without turning, he told the medic, "Evacuation hospital."

As the medic began making out Emergency Medical Tags, he asked me, "Ralph, can you go over to C Troop? There's a show in the mess hall. Get the ambulance driver."

I put on my fatigue cap and started running. The sooner the Japanese man got to a hospital, the sooner he would receive treatment. Then I started to slow down. *Never run*, someone instructed me my first day on ward duty. *And don't panic. It takes a long time for a man to die.* I hurried anyway. No one else was doing anything to help him.

I stepped into the mess hall, lit only by reflection off the movie screen at the far end. I called out, "Ambulance driver?" My voice squeaked with the insecurity of my nineteen years. Gathering myself together, I deepened my voice to one of authority: "Ambulance driver!" I was surprised when someone stood and walked back. He was a replacement who'd come into the outfit just before we left the Philippines. He returned with me to the dispensary.

The Japanese man lay as I left him. Thin steam rose from the fresh blood collecting beside his neck. I shivered, aware of the cold, unheated room. His clogged throat rattled. I wondered if that was what people called the death rattle.

Assigned to the hospital weeks after hostilities ceased, I had never seen anyone injured badly. Most patients at the squadron hospital had fevers or dermatitis infections. Serious cases were given first aid, then evacuated.

The fellow with the cut nose held an enamel basin on his lap now. He had vomited over the tops of his shoes.

"We'll need two ambulances," the medic told me. "Get the other driver too."

The mess hall was lit when I went back. Someone bellowed at the projectionist, "You're running the *last* reel, jerk!"

I walked halfway down the room before calling out, "Ambulance driver!"

Several turned. "What happened? What's the matter?"

Kentuck, a tall, lanky fellow, squeezed between the chairs and came toward me.

"Hey, Ralph!" someone yelled. "What do they want two drivers for?"

"To drive two ambulances," I answered, trying to sound cool.

On our way back I told Kentuck about the accident.

He couldn't believe it. "You mean they got a Jap in *our* hospital?" He smacked his cap down on the back of his head.

The other driver met us at the door. "My ambulance is outside," he told Kentuck. "I'm taking these three guys to the Seventy-first. You take the Jap to that civilian hospital up the road."

And Kentuck's frown deepened as he added, "So you can come back and see the rest of the movie?" He grumbled. "And who's gonna help me carry the litter? I can't carry both ends at once, you know!"

I said, "I'll go with you."

I heard rain outside. I asked the medic, "How about a blanket to throw over him?"

The medic went to the corner. He examined three olive-drab blankets, opening them, holding them up to the light for tears in the cloth. He gave us the one most threadbare.

I laid it over the man. As we picked him up, I wondered if he weighed as much as eighty pounds.

I climbed into the back of the ambulance and hooked the left, forward end of the stretcher to the wall, then the right handle to the center strap hanging from the ceiling. Kentuck did the same with the rear end of the stretcher.

"I'll ride back here," I said. I sat down on the bench alongside the stretcher.

Still grumbling, Kentuck slammed the door shut. He seldom cursed. It had something to do with "getting saved" and not using the name of the Lord in vain.

The light was still on, and I saw myself reflected in the rear door window. My hair bristled straight out under my fatigue cap. I leaned toward the stretcher to prepare for a lurch forward. Kentuck turned off the light there and the motor started. As we pulled out of the driveway, I heard dripping. At first I thought it was rain, but then realized it came from under the swaying stretcher. The man was bleeding again. The rattle resumed in his throat, from deeper down in his bronchials. I tried to keep the stretcher from swaying; with my body I attempted to absorb the bumps and sideward swaying of the ambulance. It was like the month before, standing in the landing barge in Yokohama Bay waiting for the signal that the peace treaty was signed and our troops could land. Motoring toward shore, the flotilla of low, flat barges rocked through water that splashed over the high sides. I stood in the middle of the barge then and kept moving from one foot to the other, trying to locate that ever-shifting center of gravity beneath me.

"Gol-dern replacements," Kentuck snarled. I thought at first he meant me. "Did you hear him back there?" He meant the other driver. "'*You* take the Jap up to the hospital.' Telling me what to do! I got more discharge points than he'll ever have!"

The ambulance stopped suddenly, bumping my elbow against the wall. The guard at the camp gate told Kentuck, "You can't go twenty mile an hour down a muddy road. You'll get stuck."

"And you're not supposed to stop no ambuLANCE."

"Where you headed?"

'We're takin' some Jap to their hospital up the road a piece."

"A Jap? I thought they lost the war."

"Tell them that. Some jeep hit him. Now I got to taxi him all over town."

"You should have called Quartermasters. They take care of salvage, don't they?"

"Had my way, I'd just leave him out on the road, let somebody else worry about him."

The ambulance was moving again, along paved road now, the main highway to Tokyo.

I tightened my fist around the stretcher strap. I had passed that civilian hospital a few times. It was secluded behind tall bushes. All you could see of it was the sign with a Red Cross.

An acrid odor filled the inside of the ambulance. At first I thought it was perspiration. Then I realized it was garlic, coming from the breath of the man two feet away.

Outside was a flapping sound, like wind drying clothes on the wash line back home. I leaned forward to see past Kentuck's shoulder. It was the Red Cross flag whipping as Kentuck searched for the turn-off road.

When my eyes adjusted to the darkness, I saw the man's head rolling loose, almost as if unattached. His garlic breath wheezed and his chest writhed, as if something was trying to fight its way out but the body wouldn't release it. I hoped we would get to the hospital in time.

The ambulance left the paved highway and bounced along a dirt road. At each turn I braced my body, guiding the side of the stretcher like a pinball machine, trying to counteract the thrusts and swerves of the vehicle.

"The war's over. There won't be any more dying now," a patient had told me, a middle-aged soldier with watery blue eyes. We stood on the second floor loggia, facing down into the small courtyard of what had been a high school in southern Luzon. The classrooms had been converted into hospital wards. All activity had stopped that morning. Medics and patients alike looked toward a public-address speaker that had been connected a few days earlier to the radio, so that when the news came it could be heard throughout the wards, offices, and rooms of the hospital. For a week a cease-fire announcement had been expected, ever since news came of the atomic bombings of two Japanese cities. Added to that was the threat of further bombing unless Japan surrendered unconditionally.

The radio voice carried mostly static. And then down in the courtyard a slight cheer arose, sounding more embarrassed than exuberant. It was followed by lukewarm applause.

Having just come overseas, I imagined an armistice would be greeted with hysterical joy. But veterans seemed to respond to such news with restraint and not a little skepticism. I could not make out the words until someone readjusted the radio dial and the message was repeated. "The Voice of America sends you the grand tidings: The war is over!"

That was when the fellow leaning over the wooden railing next to me turned and said, with a grin, "Thank God! The war's over! There won't be any more dying now." He reached out and shook my hand, and we congratulated each other on surviving it.

I had been drafted out of college while taking pre-med. I planned to go back after the war to become a doctor, if a medical school accepted me.

One of my professors asked me, "What reason will you put on your application?"

I thought a moment, and then said I wanted to help people. He didn't let me finish. "Don't ever tell them that. They'd reject you for certain. Tell them you're good at lab work. Methodical. Or that you think medicine is a pleasant way to make a comfortable living. And if someone in your family has an incurable disease or is crippled, mention that, too. But never tell them you want to save lives."

"Why not?"

"That kind of vocation is temporary, and they know that. It helps, too, if your father is a doctor."

The ambulance slowed suddenly, then cruised quietly. Rain peppered the roof, obscuring both sides of the road.

Kentuck yelled out his open window. We were across from the hospital and a man who understood English ran over. He wore horn-rimmed glasses and a long white smock, spotted with rain. He said he was the pharmacist. After Kentuck said that we had a Japanese civilian in the ambulance, the long gate was pulled open. Kentuck eased the vehicle into a narrow driveway, pulling up to the emergency entrance.

Together, we lifted the stretcher away from the wall. As we lowered it, the injured man's right arm, lying on the sideboard, dropped, but swung automatically back to his side on the stretcher. His being able to control the movement showed me he was not completely unconscious.

Following the pharmacist, Kentuck and I carried the stretcher into a small waiting room furnished with a desk and two dark leather couches.

The injured man's cough had sunk so deep now, it was hardly audible.

Hospital employees crowded around the stretcher to stare at him while the pharmacist questioned Kentuck about the accident. Kentuck told him the man was driving a cart without lights when a jeep hit him. Their heads rose. They all recognized the word "jeep."

The pharmacist searched the man's pockets for identification. He found a thin, folded strip of rice paper with orderly columns of Japanese script down one side. The pharmacist flashed a smile. "He is bandage-carrier," he said. I wondered if the irony amused him. Everything he said seemed followed by the same benign smile.

Someone summoned four short, plump nurses. They shuffled in, bowing to Kentuck and me before turning to the pharmacist for orders. All wore baggy trousers, blouses, and low-heeled shoes. Their caps reminded me of American sailor caps, some white, others tan or brown, each sewn with a tiny Red Cross on the front.

Finished with his questions, the pharmacist thanked us, and then spoke to the nurses. They picked up the stretcher and began to scoot out the door.

"Hey, wait!" Kentuck started after them. "Hold that right there!" Seeing that they didn't understand, he told the pharmacist, "We got to take that litter back with us and the stretcher."

The pharmacist seemed to have exhausted his English vocabulary. Retaining the remnant of a smile, he looked at us quizzically as the nurses hurried away with the stretcher.

Kentuck followed them with me a few paces behind, into the ever-darkening interior of the hospital.

We could hardly see them. We heard only their excited voices and the soft shoes shuffling along the floor. I wished I could have told them not to panic, but to keep calm and think clearly.

At each turn in the hallway, the nurses hesitated. They seemed unfamiliar with that section of the building. Maybe they were lost.

We followed them down one dim corridor after another, then outside through lightly falling rain, up a ramp, and then inside again.

I tried to memorize the path. In my mind I mapped the turns in case later we might have to find our way out alone.

"Where are they?" Kentuck kept asking me. "Where'd they go? Now what'd they stop for?"

We followed, sometimes only the sound of their shuffling feet through more hallways and more ramps. Ahead was an electric clock, and under it, a rack holding small, bulging bags, possibly patients' belongings. We saw no patients, only closed doors. From all we saw, the entire hospital could have been empty.

Another turn, another hallway, then ahead, total darkness. The nurses had stopped.

Someone was coming from behind us. We both looked around. Light outlined the figure of a man approaching, just as the light must have outlined our two figures to the nurses ahead. Like the pharmacist, this man wore horn-rimmed glasses and a long white smock, but was older than the pharmacist.

Kentuck told me, "I don't like this at all."

The nurses set the stretcher on the floor. One was fumbling with a padlock and chain that held together the handles of two white sliding doors.

Kentuck went to them and struck a match. He held it while the nurse fitted a key into the padlock. After they slid the two doors open, the first nurse opened another door to the left. A second nurse hurried into the room. She slid open another set of doors opposite, then switched on the light. We were in a small operating room, all white equipment and cement floor. The four nurses lifted the stretcher and trudged with it to a small table in the center of the room. They laid the stretcher on the examination table and then removed the raindrop-spotted army blanket covering the man.

One of them opened his shirt, baring his skinny chest. Round his neck he wore a pouch and, inside that, a wallet. While the first nurse searched his wallet, the other three trained their eyes on Kentuck and me, watching for any change in our expressions. It was only when the first nurse found and withdrew paper money from the wallet that I realized what they had suspected. I was relieved his money was still there.

The second nurse undid his trousers. A large label was sewn inside his fly. She read it aloud to the nurses. Whatever it said made the nurses snigger and try to conceal their laughter behind their fists.

The older man with horn-rimmed glasses was apparently a doctor. He went to the table and spoke at the injured man's ear. The only reply he received was a gurgle. But even that encouraged me. It seemed he understood and was trying to speak. Using a thumb, the doctor pushed first one eyelid up, then the other.

The nurses scurried around the room in short, animated steps. With what looked like squares of gray linen, dingy from being laundered too often, one nurse cleaned blood from the man's face and neck. The first nurse broke open a glass ampule and, using but one hand, managed to drain its contents into a tiny hypodermic syringe. With her other hand she pinched a loose fold of skin over his left breast, just above his heart. She punctured slowly, easing the needle in. She angled the syringe until the needle was clearly outlined under his skin, and then injected the solution. After removing the needle, she rubbed a fresh square of gray linen over the puncture spot and pinched his skin repeatedly to speed absorption. She massaged the area with her bare fingers. It struck me as unsanitary, but I supposed the danger of infection was secondary to saving his life.

A few minutes later the doctor walked back to Kentuck and me. He removed his glasses to blow a speck of dust off, and then replaced them. His smile duplicated the pharmacist's. He asked Kentuck where the accident exactly happened.

Kentuck remained silent. I answered for him. I told the doctor we didn't know; we weren't there, only at camp when an ambulance brought him in. Like Kentuck, I wanted to disclaim any responsibility.

"Dank you." The doctor nodded, dismissing us.

Kentuck gestured toward the table. "We got to take that litter and the stretcher. It belongs to us."

The doctor went to the nurses and spoke to them quietly. All four hurried out the door, leaving us alone with the doctor.

Kentuck told him, "We ain't leaving without it. That's government property."

The doctor indicated the table with his head and tapped his temple. What he said was obscured by the rattling operating table being rolled through the doorway. He apparently said the man had a brain concussion. His bland smile was the same as the pharmacist's, not wistful, not mocking or even ominous as in American war movies, merely matter-of-fact. "Soon," he said, "he will die."

His smile and those words seemed disconnected from each other. Kentuck's jaw dropped open, and his eyes darted to the right, then left, like someone trapped.

"What did you say?" I asked the doctor.

Still smiling, he repeated: "Soon he will die."

Kentuck backed away. Under his breath he muttered, "Let's get out of here."

"What about the stretcher?" I asked.

Kentuck told the doctor, "I'll be back tomorrow. I . . .will . . .come . . .tomorrow. Understand? For that-there litter. You can keep it for now."

The doctor smiled again and bowed. "Dank you."

Kentuck was already out of the room and striding along the hall. I hurried after him.

He didn't slow down. "You see that look? A cat with a mouse. Snap to, boy! Let's move it! Nobody knows we're here. These here Japs could say we never even come. They could say anything. Let's get out of here!"

I tried to make him slacken his pace by not keeping up with him, but he walked faster. "We could wait," I said, "for the stretcher." I wanted to see if they could save the man.

"I'll pick it up tomorrow. I'll bring along a couple of other guys, too. You won't catch me coming back here alone. I don't trust them as far as . . . ." His pace slowed after the first turn, and then he stopped. He looked at the walls. "This the right way? Did we come by here? I don't recognize none of this!"

I had to lead the rest of the way.

After we passed the rack of bundles stored on shelves beneath the electric clock, I said, "I know where we are now."

A nurse approaching us in the dark corridor halted. She came to attention and gave us a sharp military salute.

From the exit the pharmacist accompanied us to the ambulance, bowing and displaying his cryptic smile.

Kentuck told him, "Somebody'll be here tomorrow, me or somebody else, to get the litter. Be sure and have it. The blanket, too. By the front door, you hear?"

The pharmacist nodded. He bowed, thanking us again, as we drove off. I rode in front with Kentuck on the way back.

He said, "When they took us up that dark hallway, they would have knocked us off for sure, if they thought they could get away with it. We was lucky to get out alive."

"I think they just wanted to move him into surgery as soon as possible."

"You don't know Japs like I do. I fought them; I know how they do."

Along the dirt road ahead a boy was riding a bicycle. A long orange-colored lantern with a candle inside swung from the handlebars. Others carried round, flickering lanterns along the sides of the road. Kentuck honked his horn and gunned the motor to frighten them and see them scatter.

"Look-a-there how they walk. You can't hardly see them. No wonder the guy got hit."

A quiet shower was falling now, dwindling by the minute. When I first arrived in the Philippines four months before, I was surprised that rain looked and felt the same as in Pennsylvania. And again here in Japan. I somehow imagined rain would differ in each country, like plants and animals, and people, their languages. It was a revelation to find rain the same all over the world.

Kentuck was still muttering. "We should have dumped him, just propped him outside their gate, blowed the horn, and left. And took back the litter."

The palms of my hands were sweaty. I wished I could have washed them before we left the hospital. They stuck together when I rubbed them. In the dim light from the dashboard I saw the creases lined in red. I rode the rest of the way with my hands half-open.

The man would be in surgery now. They would be operating to save his life. Even though the doctor held little hope, they would try.

"I hate them," Kentuck said. "I hate all of them!" His fist pounded the steering wheel.

"He was just a workman," I said. "He wasn't even a soldier. He was a bandage-carrier."

"Still a Jap, though. I'd kick him—all of them—in the face if I could. All of us in battle would have. One false move and blooey! Some trigger-happy guard'll swear the whole Jap army is chasin' him, and he'll shoot ever' one of them in sight. Mark my word, you'll see it happen."

"But the war's over now."

"Not till they ship me back home. Not till I step off the train in Lou'ville. It sure in hell better be soon, too."

He frowned through the windshield, seeming unaware that the rain had stopped, although the wipers continued, back and forth. "I had my fill of them. Even their smell. You smell that powder around camp? That's how a cave full of Japs smelled that we blowed up in the jungle. That perfume and powder they use, it pert near knocked me over, that smell."

The ambulance lurched onto paved road, the one coming from Tokyo. We rode in silence, searching for road signs in English that gave the distance in miles to and from camp.

"I think that doctor can save him," I said. "He looked like he could."

"You must not have been listening. He said that is one dead Jap!"

"But the body hangs onto life. Since he was able to hang on this long, he has the will to . . . ."

"You call them human?"

"No matter how much you hate them . . . ."

"Don't you think they hate us too, as much as we hate them? Even more? We bombed the tarnation out of their country. We wiped out whole cities of theirs off the map. If it wasn't for that atomic bomb, we'd still be fighting them." He glanced over. "Boy, you still living in grade school. You never seen how evil, how downright ornery and evil they can be. I mean what they done. To civilians, too, not just GIs. To women and kids."

I nodded. "I heard."

"How they set fire to a hut, and then shoot people when they come running out. Humans? Ha! Well, I got even. I picked me off a few, too." He frowned at the road ahead, swerving to avoid pitfalls. Then turning to me, he grinned. "I kilt me a major once, a genuine officer, before they transferred me to the medics. I was driving trucks then. These Japs—four, five—come out of the hills, carrying a white flag. The one leading them was dressed real fancy. Officer, I figure. A major. Maybe even higher. So I took a bead on him and let him have it. Pow! One less Jap."

"He wasn't armed? You mean they were surrendering?"

"So what? They could have been booby-trapped. Try and help a injured Jap and they pull the pin out of a grenade. I seen that happen down in Leyte. They would toss a Flip kid up in the air, too, and catch him on the end of their bayonet. That's how they are. I'm not making this up. And if they found some woman was gonna have a baby, they'd rip her belly open and pull it out, kill them both."

I wanted to disbelieve the stories. I wanted to regard this as the same sort of propaganda we saw in war movies, where the enemies always were portrayed as bloodthirsty monsters, devoid of human feeling. But I heard similar tales in the Philippines, from civilians as well as GIs.

"That's why the Army's in such a hurry to get us veterans out and send us back home," Kentuck said. "We seen too much. Bring in the rookies, let them keep the peace." He nodded agreement with his words. "We been too easy on them, even when we was fighting them. The Flips know. Once, we turned some Jap over to some guerrillas up in the hills. They carry big bolo knives for cutting through jungle. They sent us back his ear." He chuckled. "That must have been the biggest piece still left."

He stopped speaking. Hunched with his elbows riding the steering wheel, against regulations, he allowed the motion of the vehicle to carry him along and appeared lost in thought. After a long time, he started to speak, but changed his mind, then said it anyway, his tone different, the voice slower. "Down in the Admiralties it got sort of out of hand, though. We caught this one sneaking into camp, trying to steal food, so we killed him. But then they hung him up on some old tree by a rope. Everyone that passed by took a shot at him. 'Course he was dead and couldn't feel nothing. I took a few shots myself. It felt good, too, like target practice, or a shooting gallery at amusement parks. Sometimes it's almost like your hate is blowing them to bits, for all they done. Only, when I come by a hour later, they was still at it. It didn't look like a person no more. A side of beef maybe. Nothin' left but shreds. And they was still carrying on, like some schoolyard game." He shook his head. Kentuck gripped the steering wheel properly now. "I thought to myself, Gol-almighty! Is this what we come to? Use skeletons for target practice? I took me a good aim and fired. I hit that dang rope and broke it. They was mighty sore for a while because I broke up the game. I pert near had me a fight on my hands. And they was supposed to be my friends too. Ha, war heroes!"

I wondered how war could release such hatred and savagery from apparently decent people on both sides. But, as Kentuck said, I was a rookie: I never experienced battle. Maybe such violence was hidden inside all of us. I didn't know. I hoped I never would.

He hunched over the steering wheel. "Man-oh-man, they better send us home fast. We seen too much."

The windshield wiper seemed to recite a jingle over and over: "Going home, going home, going home," until he switched it off.

"I lost me a good bunch of buddies in this here war," he said. "Ain't nothin' or nobody, no peace treaty or piece of paper, nothing's ever gonna bring them back." He recited the battles, like a litany for the dead: "The Marianas, the Admiralties, Cebu, Tacloban, Leyte, Luzon . . . ."

I nodded, not understanding or agreeing, just acknowledging indisputable facts. Maybe to kill was the only logical response in battle, the only way to survive. And if you stopped to consider the morality, it was too late. I was thankful I never had to make that choice. Yet, to kill without feeling in war seemed cleaner; hatred somehow tainted it.

Knowing Kentuck's religious bent, I wondered how he reconciled hatred with his philosophy. I tried to sound flippant. "They say every man is your brother. 'Love thy neighbor,' huh?"

"When you away from home, you ain't got no neighbors."

His finger went to the right then, a sign. "There! See? Camp, two miles."

Wisps of steam came up from the pavement where rain had cooled the sun-drenched roads from the afternoon. Fog shapes rose about four or five feet, hunched over like smoky figures; they drifted without footing across the highway. The fog earlier must have obscured the road when the jeepload of soldiers smashed into the cart. That old Japanese man had survived years of bombings and war, only to be hit by a jeep two months after hostilities ceased. His family was probably home waiting for him, not even guessing he was on an operating table, fighting for his life. And the doctor said, "Soon he will die." I would remember those words and his odd smile the rest of my life.

I clamped my hands together then, fingers interlocked, and they stuck that way. I prayed privately: Please, God! Please don't let him die!

Both Captain Jackson and the Japanese doctor said that soon he would die. Next day I learned that he did.

After Hiroshima

Liz Dolan

Shikata ga nai
 August 15, 1945

Each day in school we vow to die
for Hirohito, file past his icon with eyes cast down
as if nine suns might blind us. Even in dreams
his white wings blaze. When we hear his voice
      —an ordinary voice like any other –
            It can't be helped
we are struck dumb except for Rika who mimics it exactly
      —a twelve-year-old in tattered shorts
            speaks with the voice of a deity—
Now dry-mouthed
we fear rutted stones in a dismal swamp,
fear tears slipping into rank tea,
      —fear fear itself—
Broke like bent reeds,
we wish to extinguish ourselves
as the golden kite
                        spirals
                              to the quivering earth,
as the chrysanthemum's petals crimp brown.

Small Fires—Nagasaki
Elisabeth Murawski

The wind when it comes
is warm. There is no home
that isn't leveled

or burning. She barely
feels the tug
on her nipple, or sees

the blue-white dribble
on her baby's chin,
his swollen belly,

the one tree
left standing, its trunk
and branches a Y

incision, its few leaves
whispering
like witches. Leaning

by itself on the sky,
the gate of the temple
resembles pi,

an irrational number.
Small fires flicker. Empty,
she lets him suckle,

the child in her arms
who may die
or live without her.

The Two Things I Wanted
~ Robert McGowan ~

I got home about four months before Jerry Lebeau came back a hero. And I do think what he did in Vietnam was really wonderful, no question. I thought then and I think now that the attention he got for it was exactly what should have happened.

But what a contrast. Me, when I got back—the same town, practically the same neighborhood—it's like I'd only been away at school or something. No one thought much of it. People don't see nurses as going through anything really dramatic or troubling. We're not out tromping around in the boonies with M16s, so we're supposedly back somewhere far from the action, in some clean and neat air-conditioned hospital, taking temperatures and telling patients when to swallow their pills. Which, for many of us, if you're interested in the real truth, was about as far as you can imagine from what the situation was really like. Believe me: my experience over there was a very real war experience, as real as it gets.

As a girl growing up I wanted two things. I wanted to be a nurse and I wanted to serve my country. So I went to nursing school and then pretty soon into the Army.

In the usual civilian hospital situation Stateside, in a city of any size, you expect to see maybe one or two gunshot wounds come through on a weekend. In school and in the little working experience I had right after, this is what we were used to. But in Vietnam you could get fifty or sixty of these in one day. And not nice clean bullet wounds, either. Some of the most horrible things you could ever see.

I was up north in Chu Lai at the 312th Evacuation Hospital when I first got in country. They were short of OR people there, so they made me kind of an OR nurse, which is what I was when I worked in the States at Fitzsimons Army Hospital before Vietnam. I learned right away at Chu Lai that one of the nurses there, a girl a little older than me, was killed by a mortar round only a few weeks before I arrived on base. I hadn't thought of that happening to nurses. I think it was at that point I knew I'd gotten into a good deal more than I expected. And then, too, I was starting to see all these young guys coming in, a lot of them literally blown to pieces. The reality of it. I wasn't prepared. But I was at Chu Lai for no more than about two months. And then for my last ten months or so, they sent me farther south to the 8th Field Hospital at Nha Trang. Which for some stupid reason I thought might be better than Chu Lai. Or maybe I was just hoping so. But it wasn't.

For one thing, we actually got hit more at Nha Trang than up at Chu Lai. Of course, after a while you do get used to the mortar and rocket attacks. Which is hard for people to believe, but it's true. It was mostly a matter of only two or three explosions at a time anyway. And usually there's some warning an attack is coming—sirens and parachute flares going up—and you have bunkers all over that you can get into. Charlie was just pestering us, is what was mostly going on. Sure, you'd now and then have somebody take a little shrapnel, some building gets torn up, maybe once in a long while somebody gets killed, but, like I say, for some very odd reason you really can get pretty laid back about the mortars. I'm sure it was part of what kept us tense a lot of the time, but after a while it didn't scare you anymore like it did at first.

A whole lot worse than any of that was the horror you had to deal with every day, more heartbreaking than any normal person could take for long, things you could never, not in your whole time there, get used to in the way you get used to the mortars. In Nha Trang it was endless, maybe eighteen-hour days, longer sometimes, hardly ever a break, and this perpetual stream of the most hideous tragedy. It's upsetting for me even now, thinking about this. You have to be able to tell your mind to leave it alone, go on to something else. I had to get good at doing that. You have to or you simply can't survive, then *or* now. You'd go crazy.

By the time I'd been down in Nha Trang for a while I'd become very bitter. Full of anger. All of this ghastly horror and death, and I couldn't see anything being gained from it, all of it totally pointless. So many of the soldiers were barely more than children, really. For me, it's their eyes. All these years later I still see them. They'd look up at you like dying puppies, scared and uncomprehending. There were times when all we could do with some of them was kill their pain and let them go so we could get to the ones we might be able to keep alive. These, the ones there was no hope for, they'd know they were dying, many of them, and all they wanted was to have someone with them. Some of them crying, some just staring at nothing, some talking nonsense . . . . Three times I had them die holding my hand, one time so tight another nurse had to pry the kid's fingers away when we finally lost him. And let me make one thing clear: this is not like the movies, where some tough made-up John Wayne character gets shot and he's all stoic and in control and talking like a poet until he keels over, still looking good. That, I'm here to tell you, is pure disgusting bullshit. It's not like that. What it's like is you've got people brought in shrieking, terrified, writhing in the most godawful pain. Or so doped up with morphine that they might as well be gone already. I hate those movies, all that phony John Wayne shit. I hate that stuff more than you can possibly know. No movie shows what really happens. Unspeakable things. Guys with their legs gone . . . . I had one with barely anything left below the navel and he was still alive, still talking, for maybe a minute anyway, acting like he'd be okay. Land mine. One with his eyeballs hanging out of his skull like some gruesome monster. I've seen them with no face left, only a mass of bloody slop in place of one, and still not dead. I've seen them with every limb gone, nothing but a trunk. That's the reality. That's the reason I hate that lamebrain Hollywood John Wayne crap so much it makes me shake. Him and all like him, they're outright liars.

With the minor wounds, we'd just fix them up and send them back out into the field. With those others, though, the ones left with mangled bodies, or practically no real body at all, everything gone, eyes, faces, no legs, no genitals . . . it's hard to admit this—I'm a nurse, I'm supposed to save lives no matter what—but you want them to die. You really do hope for that. For them. It would be better. You think, *Why am I saving them, sending them home to their mothers like this, their babies grotesquely mutilated, barely anything left of them? They're just horrors now, no real resemblance anymore to a human being. Why am I doing this?* For their sakes, for their family's sake, for everyone's, you want them to die.

For a while when I got back home, I'd have flashbacks. The kind where you're not only remembering but actually re-experiencing some situation, or maybe a combination of events you'd been through, so that in a very real way you're right there again, physically, you're seeing it, you're smelling it, you're hearing it. Or nightmares—all the blood, the screaming, some frantic scene you're transported back into again . . . and it's so *hot* in those dreams . . . you're pouring sweat, you're drowning in it, you can't breathe. You see their faces, these dying kids, or what's left where their faces used to be. Even now—however long it's been, thirty-some years, almost forty; incredible—I'll have something like this come back into me once in a while. A flashback, a dream . . . . Not as pronounced as years ago, but still. . . . This stuff does not go away. It takes up residence in you. Like some foreign mass lodged in your body. It's there and it'll always be there.

I was still in the Army for a while after I got back. I was on leave for a few weeks at home but then was stationed at Brooke Army Medical Center in San Antonio. I'd already decided to get out of the Army. I couldn't deal with it anymore. At Brooke I saw what we'd sent home, all those unfixable, shattered human beings, disfigured, like a house of horrors. It was just more of the same. All so completely hopeless and depressing. There they were, more coming in all the time, and there they'd be, indefinitely, most of them, for the rest of their lives, if you can call them really alive. Out of sight and forgotten. There they were thirty years ago, and there they are right now today. And who sees it? Nobody wants to see it, which is understandable, but every adult American should be made to look. This is what war does and this is what war is and you better be damn sure it's worth it, which it almost never is. I'm still bitter. And I'm proud I'm bitter. What kind of person would I be if I weren't? I don't want to be around people who can know about this and not despise the fools among us who cause it, not only the politicians, but also the simpletons who buy into their gung-ho crap. I'm still angry. I'll always be angry.

The Vietnam experience, and then at Brooke Medical, all that suffering . . . . I had to change some things about myself after that. You might think it's nothing, but it's not nothing, it's something: I stopped eating meat, stopped being a part of slaughter. This is one arena of suffering and death I can have control over. There's misery enough in this world without my causing any more of it. I came to understand there was no good reason for killing and eating animals, just like there was no good reason for all the killing in Vietnam. The same blind stupidity. I had to stop having anything to do with killing.

I could no longer be around any kind of pain. I left the Army when my commitment was up after a few months, and I went back home to Nebraska to stay. I never went back to nursing. Through the father of a friend of mine, I got a job as secretary to the principal of the high school here. A girl Friday, as much as I hate the term. But I'm still there and it's been okay. For a long time I worked a whole lot harder than I really had to, kept looking for more to do. I see now I was trying to keep Vietnam out of my thoughts, trying to bury my feelings.

Back in the real world, with no one around anymore who had any comprehension of what you'd come out of over there, there wasn't anyone you could really talk to about it. It was another planet to them, the whole Vietnam experience. Another planet, another universe. They couldn't relate. Most Vietnam veterans will tell you the same thing. And yet you're not all that drawn to be around the vets, either, because all that does is help keep you in the Nam. So you feel isolated. I remember sitting down for lunch one day with one of the teachers, a woman not far from my own age, just the two of us, and I mentioned one or two things, some memories that had come to mind. I suppose, to be honest, I was hoping for some level of sympathy, the sense that someone would understand the weight of how I felt. But nothing. It's the most incredible thing. What I was saying to her simply didn't register. You could see it in her eyes. I wasn't connecting with her at all, almost like she was physically deaf to it. She mumbled some version of *It must have been awful*, some platitude you could see she wasn't really feeling at all, like she was only trying to put an end to any talk along those lines. So I shut up about it and we went on to whatever subject came up instead. It was a peculiar feeling. And, to be honest, hurtful. As though I'd been shunned. What I had to talk about, what I'd done, what I was, didn't matter to her.

I remember all that hoopla about Jerry's return. I don't mean I resented it in any way. I didn't, not for a single second. What he did over there, standing up to that murdering CO of his, I was proud of him for that. So I'm proud also of that granite memorial they put up to honor him. Jerry was someone who stood up against killing, stood up the best way he could with what power he had under the circumstances. He absolutely was a hero, a real one.

Me, I'm not a hero. What I am is someone who went through more than I could handle very well and then couldn't keep working in a profession I wanted to love but that reminded me every day of too many unbearable things. I'm one of thousands and thousands of both men and women whose lives were changed, and not in very good ways, by the whole criminal catastrophe of that heinous war. And remember: our losses in that war were miniscule compared to what happened to the Vietnamese, what we did to them, somewhere around three million or so killed, who knows how many ruined for life, all the environmental devastation we caused in their country. Not many people want to face up to that. I spent a long time being angry at America. I still see Vietnam as a contemptible episode. An obscenity. I wish I could say I had nothing to do with it.

I rarely ever talk about Vietnam anymore, not to anyone. It's been so long, I don't think many people around here even know I was there. But what the heck. Right?

What the heck.

They can't put up a big granite memorial in the middle of town for every one of us.

Insanity is Contagious
~ Kristin Aguilar ~

She stares past her own reflection in the mirror. She has an urge to scream, just to see if he will even notice. But she stifles it, thinking wildly that no scream could be as loud as the silence in the room. He sits stone-faced as always, locked in his private hell. The visions and auditory hallucinations he experiences are made worse by his pride and shame, both almost tangible by the duration and severity of his depression.

She stares into her own face and remembers when he told her about reading the Bible upon arriving home, desperate to find proof that all the killing he had done would not damn him. He searched the Book, trying to separate the man he had become, the man the Marine Corps had created, from men like John Wayne Gacy and Jeffrey Dahmer. She nearly giggles, musing that he probably hadn't eaten any Iraqis.

That's ridiculous, she thinks. I shouldn't be so insensitive.

She remembers the children he killed, the decision he made that came down, in essence, to the lives of his men versus those three Iraqi children. She sees their faces sometimes even though she wasn't there. She thinks she can almost taste the diesel fuel he smells constantly. She thinks of the kills he made and of his own narrow escapes. She sends a prayer up to a Private she has never met, asks him to please stop haunting her husband. His guilt has consumed him. He swore it was his fault because he sent that soldier—practically a child—into an Iraqi home first. It seems silly to her, all that second guessing and the what-ifs. The guilt seems so unearned. One of those

Marines was destined to die that day and it just so happened to be a Private her husband felt himself responsible for. Team leader, he told her. It was my responsibility.

She nearly giggles again.

Insanity is contagious.

She wants to scream—the rage, the guilt, the grief burning in her chest. But her face belies no emotion. Flat affect, the psychologist told her. He'd given her a name for the terrifying expression on her husband's face that day in late July. His face blank, eyes dead. There was no other way to describe it. A walking corpse.

She remembers the icy fear his expression had given her, and shivers. She believed then that suicide was not her husband's only option. It could be homicide—he could kill her and the children. He said he loved her and would never harm his family, but the corpse that stood staring through her in the hallway that day was not her husband.

She remembers the horrible realization at that moment that this could be life or death for all of them. She remembers talking to him, lying, telling him it would be okay, that their marriage was not ending. She managed to convince him that he was suicidal, that he needed to seek immediate help in the form of inpatient treatment. It was a struggle, but he finally agreed, if only to prevent her leaving. She didn't care. She would cross that bridge later.

This time she does laugh out loud.

Behind her, in the mirror, he does not stir. He probably can't even hear her laugh over the gunfire that plays in his head. She resists the impulse to strike at him, throw things, scream to make him feel something. She shoves her rage down, back into the burning hole in her chest. She tries to remind herself how ill he is, how desperately sick this man has really become. She wishes he'd gotten the help he needed long ago when it could have made a difference. But she pushes that idea away as well. Regrets and wishes now are futile.

She smiles again. Futile. What a funny-sounding word.

Insanity is contagious.

She hates him for the pain he's caused her and continues to cause her. She pities his private hell but rages at him for dragging the rest of them down. She rages at God for allowing her husband to come home from Iraq only to die this way. She grieves for the man she loved, for the marriage that should have been, for the dreams she used to believe would come true. She thinks of the woman she once was and grieves for those pieces now gone. She has the insane and childish urge to scream violently about how unfair it has all been.

She hates.

She hates the Iraq war, the government for abandoning her husband, and the Marine Corps for instilling that sense of pride which kept him trapped in his darkness for so long. She hates him for the man he has become and herself for wanting to be happy. She wonders how a person reaches the point where hating herself for wanting to be happy makes any sense.

Insanity is, indeed, contagious.

She stands before the mirror, broken and afraid, seeing herself as a trembling mass of unexpressed emotion. She gazes at her reflection for a full minute, realizing that she has finally reached the critical moment. She can continue this way, dying a little bit inside every day, or not. So, decision time has arrived. It is time to live or die.

Images pass through her mind: the hospitals, the ambulance, the doctors, the medications, the handgun at her husband's temple. His darkness had become her darkness, and she now stands a hair's breadth away from crossing the threshold of his hell. If she falls in with him, there will be no hope for their beautiful children. She had made sure he was okay, had saved his life over and over. Now what?

She turns from him, from their room and their home and the darkness therein, her sense of self-preservation just winning over the guilt of abandoning him. He watches as she backs away from that threshold, both pain and relief obvious on his face. He is more comfortable in the sanctuary of his private hell.

She had hoped someday he would be able to save himself.

Later she will reflect on that moment. She will lie in the bathtub, away from the eyes and ears of the children, and release her pain in gulping sobs. But, ultimately, she will move on, as she has to, bringing the children back into the light with her. She will remember her turmoil and her weakness, the despair and the fear. But she will remember most of all a strength in herself she did not know she possessed.

She will live.

Flamethrower
Diane Judge

In Nam
I did not inch along
seeking sly attrition.
I launched horror full-on
with a jellied juggernaut,
grafted pain
on province and person,
stripped foliage and flesh,
burned last breaths
from uncounted
pairs of lungs.
The napalm I used
knew no nuance.
Even now,
in recurrent dreams
it ignites
my own screams.

A Veteran's Interview Concerning Agent Orange and Cancer
~ Henry F. Tonn and Robert McGowan ~
Based on an original interview with Robert McGowan by Steve Hussy of Meridian Star Press

Tell us about the cancer you've contracted.

I was diagnosed in January of this year, 2012, with a non-Hodgkins lymphoma, B-cell, stage II. I have a wad of college degrees but not much interest in medical matters, so I haven't really learned much about it. It's my understanding that non-Hodgkins lymphoma is a cancer generally susceptible to treatment, but mine is being stubborn.

Does the Veterans Administration have compensation policy for this?

The VA does have a "compensation" policy in place now for these kinds of problems. If a Vietnam veteran contracts a kind of cancer they have determined is connected to Agent Orange exposure, then they behave toward the vet as though he/she deserves something from them, so they "compensate" the victim with a monthly payment during treatment, and for six months afterward if the veteran survives. So I'm getting some money each month, which does help financially, though, on the whole, I'd rather not be seeing them at all with this problem. Aside from the fact that the lymphoma might kill me, it has made my life miserable. The side effects of treatment include weakness, lack of energy, and difficulty concentrating, to name a few, not to mention the frequent and long hospital stays.

What is the relationship between Agent Orange and cancer?

Agent Orange-connected cancers are increasingly common among Vietnam vets, far more common than among the general population, so there's really little doubt that, in my case, given there's virtually no history of cancer in my family going back several generations, and given that I've never been exposed to any other cancer-causing material, and given that Agent Orange was, in fact, widely used where I was in Nam, it's pretty near certain my cancer is Agent Orange-connected, a delayed gift from Uncle Sam, the American military, and Dow Chemical Company, among various other manufacturers of that hideous poison.

What about Agent Orange and the Vietnamese people?

The horrors of Agent Orange are far worse in Vietnam than among American veterans of that war. Several million Vietnamese have suffered grisly illness and death because of the Agent Orange sprayed over a high percentage of their country, and over a half-million babies there have been born either dead or with grotesque birth defects. And these effects are not going away. The United States has done practically nothing to aid the Vietnamese in this tragedy. We haven't even legally acknowledged that we're the source of this mess.

What is the treatment and how are you progressing?

The usual treatment is chemotherapy and radiation. I was to receive six chemotherapy treatments to be followed by several sessions of radiation. This, I anticipated, would cure me. However, a CT scan taken after my fifth chemo treatment indicated that my tumor had not responded. It had, in fact, grown through those few months. So we've skipped the radiation and I've gone through three three-day, inpatient chemo treatments with a more aggressive chemo regimen than my previous one. So far, that isn't working either. Next is stem cell transplant. My odds have gone from ninety per cent positive to thirty per cent positive. It's not looking good.

How does stem cell transplant work?

I don't know much about it except that there are various kinds of stem cell transplants. I'm getting a kind that requires a donor. It has to do with strengthening one's immune system, I think, so that, with an accompanying rough-tough chemo, the cancer will no longer be able to live in me.

How do you feel about the prospect of dying?

I would say I have little emotion about dying. I'd rather not do it, of course, but I'm not afraid of it. My greatest source of pain is the grief this will cause my beloved wife, Peg, and the rest of my family and friends. Also, I have a lot of writing not yet published. This I do care about very deeply. I am my work. I want my work to live and I want to live to work.

Is it possible to have complete proof that your cancer is due to Agent Orange?

No. It's hard to prove it legally or otherwise. Consequently, the chemical companies who manufactured Agent Orange have kept largely out of trouble (legal responsibility) for many years now. Despite what is widely considered clear evidence that Agent Orange has had horrendous effects on many Vietnam War veterans and innocent Vietnamese civilians, not one of the manufacturers or users of this substance has been proven liable.

How do you feel about the people who manufactured and defend Agent Orange?

Well, in this case, it took two to tango. Dow Chemical and others manufactured the drug, but the United States Government used it. I might be dying because of the collaboration of those two. How do you *think* I feel about them?

Faith

Diane Judge

For Linwood Earl

Hook laced with Agent Orange,
Vietnam reels me in.
I wriggle free,
swim back toward the world.

Sleeper cells lie dormant,
awaken when I'm fifty-four,
cluster in a bump on my shoulder.
Tentacles adhere to every organ.

Once elusive, serenity
now eases my labored breath.
Before me lies the shore
I will wash up on.

THE LAST PRISONER

~ Louis M. Prince ~

The above facts and events were recorded by the author who was the
artillery captain visiting the Company Command Post.

On May 7th, 1945, the unconditional surrender of Germany was signed by members of the German High Command. During two and a half years of combat, beginning in North Africa and ending near the Elbe River in Germany, a United States infantry division known to many as the Old Reliables suffered 22,202 casualties. The number of casualties they inflicted on the enemy could not be counted, but the division captured about 130,000 prisoners, more than 50,000 of them in the last month of the war in Europe. There were days in that last month when so many Germans tried to surrender that some had to be asked to come back the next morning.

The last organized resistance met by the Old Reliables was during the reduction of the Harz Mountains pocket. After reaching their objectives, members of one of the division's regiments passed through a notorious German labor camp, situated at Nordhausen. Mass graves, hastily abandoned and left open, revealed emaciated corpses, including those of women and children, limbs askew and mostly naked. The emaciated living, clad in filthy garments, could barely move. Only their deep, hollow eyes seemed to speak. On April 20th, Adolf Hitler's birthday, the Harz Mountains were completely encircled by British and American forces, and resistance there ended.

The next day the Reliables were ordered to move eastward toward the Elbe River. G-2 Intelligence anticipated no further organized resistance, just mopping up and patrolling for stragglers. Everyone knew that the end was near. Sergeant Smith, a squad leader in one of the rifle companies, was very old. He was 31. He was also tough and mean to a certain extent. After enlisting in the peacetime army at age 18, the Army had become his home. He had been a squad leader in the Company since the breakthrough at St. Lo, nine months earlier, and that was a very long time for a front line infantryman to stay alive. He had seen men killed and wounded in the most gruesome ways imaginable during those nine months, men who had been his responsibility. At times a non-stoppable panorama ran through his mind: squad members decapitated by 88s, gutted by personnel mines, crushed by tanks; puddles of blood, exposed organs, severed limbs. "Ground war is always cruel beyond imagination," Norman Mailer writes. But the sergeant himself bore only a few scars from light shrapnel wounds which were treated by Company Aid men.

His squad was now miserably understrength, with replacements arriving less and less frequently with less and less training, so that it had become more and more of a challenge to shepherd the green troops through these final days of combat. About April 15th the most recent replacement had arrived, a teenager, smooth-skinned and baby-faced, except for a few pimples to proclaim his adolescence. Just a few months before he had enlisted in Mount Vernon, New York, on his 18th birthday, the same age at which the sergeant had joined up. But this kid was not at home in the Army. Awkward, skinny, of minimum height, he seemed a lost cause, and his name soon became Sad Sack II. The only compensation for his hopeless military incompetence was his radiant smile as he cheerfully tried to follow orders, while seeming incapable of understanding them. Sergeant Smith would roll his eyes and swear, as only he could swear. Yet the sergeant found himself silently vowing that, at this late date, Sad-Sack II, as well as the rest of the squad, absolutely *must* survive.

As the Company moved on eastward, still mostly in combat formation, no resistance was encountered. It was a warm, sunny afternoon as the Company passed along a slope through the edge of a carefully tended forest. Sergeant Smith's squad was on the point. Immediately behind were the company commander and his small party which included an artillery forward observer. The company commander was a grizzled veteran, age 25. He had been assigned to one of the division's rifle companies as a private first class before D-Day. Since then he had been wounded three times, captured once, yet he had always gotten back to his unit, usually by hitchhiking from the hospital. At The Bulge, he had led a few men to a vital junction that he held finally all by himself with a .30 caliber air-cooled machine gun, long enough for certain elements of the Division Headquarters to escape being trapped. For this spectacular feat he was awarded the Distinguished Service Cross, a battlefield commission, and command of his present company.

The visiting artillery observer, a captain, had been a Reliable since the early days. Artillerymen usually view their carnage from a gentlemanly distance. But when they take their turn as forward observer with the front-line infantry, they find out what combat is all about. A few days after that, if they survive, they go back to the safety of the rear, a different world.

The Company was proceeding through the woods, not entirely unwary, but with the underlying feeling that the war was over. They had heard the Russians were in Berlin. Most of the prisoners now were children in Hitler Jugend uniform and old men of the Volksturm.

To the left of the Company's sector of advance was a strip of green meadow, about 25 yards wide, sloping toward a small brook. On the far side of the brook was the same thing, a slope planted with pines and spruce not over eight feet high, apparently a nursery or preserve of some sort. This slope, behind the brook, was the sector of another unit, Company "A," but no Company "A" personnel were visible. The slope appeared vacant, though we knew it could very well serve as a screen for a sniper. But not even Sergeant Smith was contemplating further conflict. He behaved as if they were now a troop of unkempt boy scouts on a nature hike.

Suddenly, from the left, came the sound of a burp gun. The CO party dove to the ground, trying to bury themselves in the forest floor. Bullets zinged through the trees and ricocheted off stones with whining noises. A moment later rifle fire from the squad aimed in the general direction of the enemy drowned out the burp gun.

"Cease fire! You idiots are firing into Able Company's sector!" Sergeant Smith bellowed. Indeed, Company "A" personnel could now be seen in the distance.

At almost the same time the shout "Medic! Medic!" was heard, and a company aid man, crouching, scurried forward.

As soon as the rifle fire stopped, a figure sprang up from behind one of the spruces on the opposite slope. Throwing his helmet and burp gun to the ground, the man shouted, "Kamerad! Kamerad!" as he raised his arms high into the air.

The burp gun was an MP44 machine pistol, something like an American Tommy gun, but better engineered and more accurate. Magazine capacity was thirty rounds; cyclic rate of fire was eight hundred rounds per minute. A few rounds at that speed sounds like a burp. The man had just fired his last rounds.

The fire had been accurate enough to kill one man and lightly wound two others of the squad. It was our Sad Sack II who lay crumpled, his blood spurting out onto a little patch of wildflowers. Where his throat had been torn by several bullets there was a big crimson gap, so that his head hung at an odd angle, face to the ground.

"Kamerad!" repeated the German. "Allein, allein," as he continued forward toward the half-dozen Americans, rifles at the ready.

"Hold your fire, men. This one's mine," the sergeant spoke evenly, just loud enough for the squad to hear.

"Come here!" he commanded. The German approached the sergeant, who noted the black shoulder straps and collar patches of the Waffen SS. He was a tall, blonde, model "Aryan" Nazi.

The SS man came closer, stood before the sergeant and saluted.

Between them, on the ground, lay an M-1 rifle, probably the Sad Sack's. In one lightning-like motion, the sergeant grabbed the rifle by the barrel and swung it upward so that the butt struck the SS trooper's jaw—a mighty blow. The German had flinched just enough to escape the full force, but he staggered and tried to raise his arms to shield his face. Then, using the butt as a rammer, the sergeant landed a quick blow in the solar plexus area. As the SS prisoner sank, he rammed the rifle butt with all his strength into the man's face, smashing it like a piece of pottery. A few more blows and the twitching body lay quiet. The skull was broken open and elements from inside oozed onto the ground.

"Never mind the medics," he muttered as he turned away. The sun, filtered by the trees, cast a mottled pattern on the mutilated body of the German soldier.

During the beating, which was over quickly, the squad members drew back and watched, without apparent emotion. The artillery captain, ranking officer at the scene, theoretically, could have intervened. He looked at the company commander questioningly. The Lieutenant shook his head: "It's best to let them be."

Observation Post

Hugh Martin

Hanley spits strings of saliva-
laced dip into the gravel. Hours ago, a dud dropped
on the south side of the FOB, sent up a breath
of dust. Marwan, the interpreter,

drives to the entrance gate,
picks up his two boys. Their summer job:
filling sandbags for dinars.
At the intersection one mile down the road,
a three-round burst,
a precise incision
through the windshield. Neck, mouth, nose.

We drive with the captain in a Humvee
and find the two boys
crouched together, hands
over heads on the floor, their father
wet on their bodies.

Captain takes a photo, and we lean
toward the backseat window, as he points
at red scraps of Marwan,
beside the seatbelt buckle. Later,
he'll show everyone, magnifying
the camera's screen, *that's skull
right there, that's skull,*
as if needing others to agree.

We watch crowds carry the wood coffin
through Sadiyah's streets.
Peshmerga arrive in jeeps
with RPGs, Kalashnikovs;
they drag suspects
to the police station,
where they'll take turns
with the rifle butting.

I'm cleaning my fingernails with a Gerber;
Hanley whispers,
A shooting star. When I look, he says,
Go fuck yourself. Before dawn,
we see movement
in the retreating darkness. Through the binos:
a donkey mounts another in a field.
When our relief shows up, we say,
if you're bored, two donkeys
are fucking at three o'clock;
a dud hit before midnight;
Marwan is dead.

THE CHECKPOINT
~ Byron Barton ~

All Jeff ever wanted to do was get away from Vermont. Away from the leftover hippies, bitter from busted utopian dreams, seeking a bastion where some semblance of '68 could limp on. Away from the nouveau hippies, reeking of hemp and patchouli, bitter because the dream was dead and had been since before they were born. Away from his life, where arbitrary work demands and snarling yardbirds were making him as bitter and resentful as the trust-fund-ragamuffins playing bongos in the park.

In the fall of 2004, there was one sure way to get out. Volunteer for war. Simple. And it was.

Now spring was turning to summer and he was in the middle of Iraq, in the thick of a brutal insurgency. At the tip of the spear. Taking the fight to the enemy, as ethereal as they were deadly.

Jeff and nine other members of his advisory support training (AST) team were embedded in an Iraqi mechanized infantry battalion, helping with everything from logistics to building intelligence networks to raiding terrorist strongholds in the middle of the night.

"I'm about sick of babysitting jundie," Sergeant First Class Knut said to him from behind tired eyes, so blood-shot from sleep deprivation and filth it looked as if the man had conjunctivitis. A layer of grime and dust from manning a checkpoint with a contingent of Iraqi grunts, called jundie, coated Knut's uniform and gear.

Jeff nodded, wondering if he looked as bad as Knut, but knowing he didn't. At least he wasn't out in the dust and mud last night. He had spent the evening in relative luxury, in the tactical operations center, or TOC, spelling the Major at the radio, waiting for word of any activity at the checkpoints. Last night the Captain accompanied a group of jundie to a checkpoint. Tomorrow night would be Jeff's turn in the field. If he weren't required to stay up all day helping the Iraqi officers with logistics, he would be looking forward to it.

The sun was cresting the horizon, cutting through darkness and illuminating a broad expanse of freshly plowed fields, bisected by dirt roads and dry wadis, slowly gaining in elevation before terminating in a range of hills ten kilometers distant. With morning, the teams, consisting of one American, one Iraqi officer and twenty jundie, should be returning to base. Their checkpoints were set along the distant ridge, meant to catch insurgents trying to bypass Route Anaconda, a heavily patrolled road going into Tall Afar, a city of 200,000.

Tall Afar, not exactly a cultural hub under Saddam's rule, had been further battered by continuous urban warfare since the U.S. invasion a year and a half before. Now, sporadic gunfire and explosions could be heard throughout the city, around the clock, every day of the week. Civilians continued to abandon their homes on a daily basis, seeking safety with relatives in other cities or in refugee camps. Half the concrete and cinderblock houses throughout the city, even the expensive-looking mansions, were deserted: concrete skeletons in a sea of dying neighborhoods.

One by one the NCOs rolled into the American dayroom, each as dirty and tired-looking as Knut. Once they were all present and accounted for, the Major would perform an After Action Review, or AAR, after which the men could get some much deserved rest.

While they were waiting for the last of the team to arrive, men began breaking down their M4s, cleaning away the night's detritus. Clacks of metal on metal and the sounds of brass brushes scraping away oxidized cordite filled the otherwise silent room. Everyone was physically tired and mentally exhausted, not only from a night manning checkpoints, where endless boredom could be interrupted by death at any time, but also from the last six months of nights and days dealing with the challenges inherent in standing up an army from scratch, growing the battalion from less than a hundred men into eight hundred, all needing to be fed and supplied and trained.

Most of the jundie came from simple backgrounds, such as farming and construction labor. Many were illiterate. Some were patriots. Some were ex-insurgents, now fighting for the Iraqi army out of circumstance rather than any ideal. Most were motivated by the promised hundred fifty bucks a month salary and free food.

Standing by a whiteboard affixed to one side of the day room, the Major looked over his team, sitting on lawn chairs in a semicircle around the whiteboard, hard at work cleaning their weapons, elbows deep in scattered parts, blackened q-tips and pipe cleaners, CLP, and cleaning kits. All were accounted for except one.

"Sergeant Simmons back yet?" he asked the group.

A couple of the men looked up. Most remained doggedly fixed over their work, like sleep-deprived automatons. All shook their heads.

"Reaper 56, this is Reaper 6. Over," the Major said into his radio, trying to raise Simmons. "Reaper 56. This is Reaper 6. Over."

The radio remained silent.

"He was out with Captain Hashish last night?" the Major asked, confirming what he already knew.

"Yes, sir," Jeff replied. He'd broken down his M4 as well, mostly to be doing something rather than because it was dirty.

This time a couple of NCOs looked up with something bordering alarm. Mixing Simmons, a skinny little rawhide soldier who was nonetheless the most aggressive team member, with Captain Ali, aka Captain Hashish, for his propensity to see insurgents in every shadow, was like putting Alexander the Great and Genghis Khan together in an unguarded city fat with plunder and telling them to have a good time.

As if the thought was a foreshadowing of something more ominous, a deep bass wave passed through the room, as if the hand of God had reached down and slapped them in the gut.

"If I needed CPR, that might have done the trick," the Major said. Heads nodded in agreement. A couple of the men rubbed their chest and stomachs from the uncomfortable experience.

"Tall Afar?" Sergeant First Class Eves, nicknamed Gumby because of his wide shoulders and uncommonly long arms, asked.

"Could be Mosul, or anywhere in between. Probably a five hundred pounder," Jeff said. The concussion they felt was overpressure from a huge explosion, able to travel miles before attenuating into nothing.

Thirty seconds later, the door to the dayroom burst opened. Suddenly alert, the men grabbed their pistols, only to be met by the Master Sergeant and Captain, in from the TOC.

"Just got word from Simmons," the Captain said breathlessly. The TOC's radio had a longer range than the handhelds. "There's been a huge explosion down by Checkpoint 1."

Checkpoint 1 was the final checkpoint along Route Anaconda before entering Tall Afar.

A flurry of concentrated action erupted, as if a bomb had gone off in the day room. Days and weeks of accumulated fatigue disappeared in an instant. Weapons' parts flew through the air as firearms were reassembled in record time. Those who had their body armor and Kevlar helmets hastily pulled them on, while those who didn't ran to their rooms to grab them.

Outside, in the center of the compound, Iraqi soldiers also burst into frenzied action, albeit with more frenzy and less expedience. Half a dozen Iraqi UAZ's, similar to a small Jeep and called Yazzes by the Iraqis, jockeyed for position in the convoy assembling in response to radio calls from the checkpoint. Jundie ran to and fro in various states of dress. Some had full body armor while some hadn't taken the time to gear up or hadn't yet found the time. One jundie wrestled a PKM, a belt-fed machine gun, into its bracket on the roll bar of a Yaz, while two more ran across the court yard with belts of ammo sliding down their shoulders, the ends extending to their legs, tripping them up as they ran.

"Medic 1, this is Reaper 6. Over," the Major said into his radio. A total of four US medics had been assigned to assist and advise the battalion. Three Navy corpsmen ran the battalion clinic and trained Iraqi soldiers as medics, and one army medic was attached to the AST team to handle any combat casualties.

"This is Medic 1. Over," a voice responded, tense with concern at being called, yet confident in its ability to handle whatever situation might require medical attention.

Medic 1 was the senior corpsman, Senior Chief Moore.

"Roger Medic 1. There's been an explosion at Checkpoint 1 with probable casualties. Can you ready your medics and meet us down in the courtyard?"

"Affirmative, Reaper 6. We're on our way."

The Major made a second call, summoning the AST's two interpreters.

The ASTs ran down to join the jundie fracas in the courtyard, the Major assigning positions in the two up-armored Humvees on the fly. There were ten slots for fifteen people. Jeff felt sick. He was going to get left behind. Each Humvee only needed one officer and the Major and Captain would get dibs by right of rank. Jeff knew he could hardly justify kicking an NCO out of his spot just because he didn't want to miss out on the action. That's it, he thought, a sick feeling of finality settling in his gut, he was getting left behind.

In short order, the Iraqi officers and NCOs worked the jundie into a relative semblance of order, and the Iraqi convoy was on its way out. From long months of practice, the Americans were able to get their Humvees loaded and in gear in time to take positions in the departing convoy.

"Damn, L.T., what are we going to do?" Doc P., the army medic asked when it became clear they weren't going to get a seat in the Humvees. Doc P. was a good-natured, big-boned, swarthy twenty-something from Texas. He reminded Jeff of Hoss, from *Bonanza*.

"I have the keys to the ambulance," Doc Row, short for Arrow, replied. As the junior corpsman, it looked as if he was going to be denied a seat in the Humvees as well.

"The hell with it. Let's go," Jeff said. Like a trio of teenagers at an amusement park, the three enthusiastically ran for the Iraqi ambulance. It was an old-school design, looking like the Mystery Machine from Scooby-Do, only painted a uniform light brown, with the Red Crescent emblazed on the side. Since the ambulance lacked armor, they would be exposed to roadside bombs and bullets, but it was better than being left behind. Ambulances were supposed to be exempt from hostile action under the Geneva Convention but insurgents generally weren't up on their wartime laws and proper fighting ethics.

Jeff had a vague sense of discomfort at taking off in the ambulance without clearing it with the Major, but the Major doubtless had his hands full getting sitreps and trying to coordinate actions with the Iraqi BN commander, Lieutenant Colonel Nas.

In the span of a minute, hectic chaos descended to silence as the last vehicle left through the gate. The only remaining noise was the sound of Doc Row trying to turn over the ambulance's engine.

"We just had it started three days ago," he said under his breath, turning the key and listening to the engine grind. It wouldn't do to be too far behind the convoy, like a lone gazelle separated from the herd.

Jeff and Doc P. were already aboard and ready to go, Jeff in the passenger's seat and Doc P. in the back.

Finally, the engine sputtered to life. Doc Row gently revved the struggling engine, coaxing it to a healthy roar before releasing the clutch and lurching across the courtyard as he shifted the reticent transmission to second and then third.

The three shouted triumphantly as they flew out of the gate, ebullient in their adrenaline-induced excitement and the prospect of adventures waiting at the end of the road, naive to the horrors of war despite six months in-country and several dust-ups with the enemy. Doc Row gunned it onto Route Anaconda, causing the back end to peel out, adding to the general atmosphere of joviality, like they were sixteen again and out for a joy ride.

Three hundred meters ahead was the tail end of the Iraqi convoy. To the delight of his passengers, Doc Row buried the pedal trying to catch up.

Jeff and Doc P. had their guns pointed out the windows, the former an M4 and the latter an M16, ready in the unlikely event insurgents decided to attack. Driving in an up-armored Humvee was like being transported in a vault on wheels. Being in an unarmored vehicle with the windows down after spending so much time in the Humvees was liberating.

Doc Row quickly caught up to the convoy. The rear vehicle, an Iraqi Yaz with a PKM mounted on top, motioned him ahead, to take up a position in the center of the convoy. They could see the pair of Humvees and four or five Yazzes ahead, toward the front of the convoy.

Jeff nodded to the gunner as they passed. The Yaz's occupants were considerably more solemn than the trio, but that had little effect on their own elevated spirits. Excitement mounted the closer they came to the checkpoint.

"See anything?" Doc Row asked, concentrating on the road.

"Not yet," Jeff answered, straining to see ahead while simultaneously trying to pay attention to the flashing scenery beyond the barrel of his gun, still pointed out the window. As they approached the outskirts of Tall Afar, the countryside yielded to increasingly dense patches of houses, most constructed of mud brick or concrete. The more urbanized their surroundings, the more restricted their line of sight, increasing the potential danger. Rather than subdue their exuberant feelings, however, the extra adrenaline juiced them to a new height.

"I see some smoke ahead," Jeff said after they had traveled another kilometer or so.

"Here we go, L.T.!" Doc P. shouted excitedly, practically bouncing up and down. He reached up and clapped Jeff on his shoulder.

Rounds of laughter and hell-yeahs followed.

Another couple of hundred meters and it became apparent that Jeff's "some smoke" was actually a lot of smoke, roiling up in massive clouds, obsidian black and greasy.

Thirty seconds later the convoy was at the checkpoint. As the front vehicles pulled to a stop before a set of concrete barriers, those behind bunched together one after another. Once stopped, jundie started jumping over the sides of Yazzes. Jeff and Doc P. hurriedly jumped out of the van, leaving Doc Row to find a place to park.

Jeff walked around the front of the van and stood facing something from the Seventh Circle. If not for the Major, now out of the Humvee and motioning him up, Jeff would have stood slack-jawed at the carnage spread before him like a buffet for vengeful demons.

Jeff made his way to the Major.

To the left of the checkpoint three Yazzes were on fire, the source of the billowing smoke. In front of them, tangled in a mass of concertina wire, was a scorched engine block. Various melted and broken parts and pieces ranging from the size of a marble to a fist were scattered over the road and the parking lot, about the size of a football field, to the left of the checkpoint.

The air was tinged with a permeating, almost viscous, yellow fog, born from smoke and cordite. Bits of ash floated through the air, a final touch to the post-apocalyptic scape.

Three jundie lay prone in the road, their skin charred black, gruesome rictus exposing white teeth, identifiable as jundie only because remnants of burned-out body armor and helmets were visible. A twisted AK lay next to one of the blackened corpses. One of the dead jundie was curled into a fetal position, another's burned arm was reaching skyward, sinew and bone visible under blackened flesh, frozen in some sort of roasted rigor mortis, terminating in a bony hand of curled fingers and an index finger, pointed to the sky as if in accusation.

All three jundie were still smoking, occasional tendrils of flame leaping up when smoldering embers found a pocket of fat or flesh not yet reduced to carbon and ash.

Along the right side of the road were three or four civilian vehicles, where they had lined up to await passage through the checkpoint. Inside some, Jeff could see the outline of bodies.

In an instant, the atmosphere of bonhomie and careless adventure from the ride vanished, replaced by a dull emptiness. A melancholy wave of empathy threatened to invade the void, but Jeff pushed it back. It was better to feel nothing at all.

"VBED?" Jeff asked the Major, his voice ice.

"Looks like it," the Major said. Jeff saw the battle in the Major's eyes as he struggled to strike down any emotion from the shocking sights surrounding them. After a second, a determined hardness flooded the Major's features.

"See if you can find out the dead jundies' names," he ordered Jeff before turning to the Master Sergeant. "Master Sergeant, have the men assist with security in whatever way they can."

"Yes, sir!" the Master Sergeant replied. Scattered shots continued to pop off around the perimeter, hastily set up by Iraqi officers and NCOs in the moments after the explosion. Jeff figured less than ten minutes had passed since they were ensconced in the dayroom, looking forward to a morning of peace and quiet.

"We're going to set up a triage over there," Senior Chief Moore said to the Major, pointing to a grassy area ten meters to the right of the road.

"Roger," the Major replied, turning to find Lieutenant Colonel Nas.

Jeff walked the three meters to the dead jundie. As he walked, his boots kicked over some of the scattered debris. Some of the pieces had a strange texture, soft and pliable rather than hard and rigid like he expected. He bent down to get a closer look and realized they were pieces of meat.

"Sudan man," he heard a voice say. Jeff looked up to see Captain Raheem, the Iraqi battalion's intelligence officer. "Sudan man come and make explosion in BM." Jeff knew BM was short for BMW.

"Sudan man," Raheem continued, obviously upset. "Next time I see Sudan man, I throw them into the jail."

"Do you know the names of the dead jundie?" Jeff asked, nodding toward the fallen soldiers, still smoking and burning. There had to be some way to put out the fires but Jeff didn't want to do anything disrespectful. He wasn't sure what would be considered worse, to let the fires burn out or to spray them with a fire extinguisher or something.

Raheem shook his head no, his mind still on the track of hunting down every Sudanese in the area. Jeff didn't bother trying to explain how 99.9% of the Sudanese laborers were exactly that, trying to earn enough money to send home to their families. Jeff could only imagine such abject poverty that forced you to come to a war zone where the locals were lucky to make a hundred fifty bucks a month in order to survive.

Jeff saw Captain Hashish approaching, a fire extinguisher in hand. The man went from body to body, spraying short blasts of powdery extinguishing fluid until the smoldering flesh was quenched. Hashish was half nuts, but Jeff had to give him credit, he got the job done.

"Get me some supplies!" Jeff heard Senior Chief Moore shout. Jeff turned toward Senior's voice. Senior was running toward the triage area, carrying an eight-year-old girl in his arms, her skin greyish white. From Jeff's vantage point she looked unresponsive, her head slack, hanging down from a delicate neck, but she must have been alive or Senior wouldn't have been running. The man was visibly upset, less able or willing to compartmentalize like the rest of the team, but then his job was to save lives. Jeff knew the man had a daughter at home about the same age. That probably didn't help matters.

Five or ten other civilians in various states of injury were sitting and lying in the grassy triage area. Jeff took a second and walked down the line of civilian cars. In one there were two dead bodies in the back. The car farthest from the blast was empty, the front doors hanging open, its windows shattered, all four wheels flattened. One of the cars held a civilian man, still in the driver's seat, his head leaned back at an odd angle. Blood from a neck wound ran down onto the man's white dishdasha, forming an uneven red scarf. There was something else protruding from a gaping hole in his throat. Something grey and rubbery-looking. Something that looked slightly out of place. With a start, Jeff realized it was the man's brain, somehow knocked loose from his skull, oozing down through the pharynx and out the throat wound.

Scattered gunshots, sufficiently ubiquitous as background noise that Jeff ceased to pay them any mind, were interrupted by a sustained stream of full auto gunfire, coming from just a few feet away. Jeff jumped, and looked over to see a jundie holding a belt-fed PKM. He couldn't have been more than seventeen or eighteen, rail-thin and baby-faced, looking like a caricature of Poncho Villa with machine-gun belts strapped around both shoulders. He was standing up, firing from the hip, his finger clenched against the trigger, the receiver burning through a belt long enough to coil on the ground. The jundie's eyes were closed and tears were running down his face, cutting through a layer of dust, forming muddy streaks on gaunt cheeks.

Bullets and tracers flew from the barrel of the PKM, looking like a laser. So far they were pointed upward at a thirty degree angle, clearing jundie at the perimeter, but clearly the young soldier was no longer functioning in any sort of reality, and a slight shift of posture would send a stream of rounds into the backs of soldiers holding the perimeter.

Sergeant First Class Simmons was there in a second, grabbing the PKM while Captain Hashish tackled the man to the ground. They secured the weapon and worked to calm the jundie before walking him to a Yaz and putting him under the supervision of an Iraqi NCO.

No one seemed to harbor any ill will toward the jundie, still crying, but at least no longer a danger to anyone. No one was hurt, so there probably wouldn't be any disciplinary action. Hell, Jeff was feeling a touch of psychological disequilibrium himself. If he were ten years younger and fresh off the farm, he might be tempted to lose it, too. He wouldn't, he convinced himself, but he could see how it might happen.

Jeff looked over at Raheem. The man was still muttering something about Sudan man. Jeff needed to get the identities of the dead jundie. They were burned beyond recognition so it would have to be from someone who was on duty at the time of the explosion. No easy task, considering the psychological state of some of the jundie.

Jeff walked over to where Hashish knelt by one of the bodies, his eyes black flints.

"Any idea of their names?" he asked, enunciating clearly and speaking loudly in an effort to bridge the language barrier.

Hashish simply shook his head. As Jeff contemplated what to say next, Hashish reached over and slipped his hand under one of the corpse's burned armor. The body was still smoking slightly, or maybe it was steam, but Hashish didn't seem to care. His hand came up with an Iraqi ID card, a laminated piece of paper about the size of an index card. Hashish handed it to Jeff. The ID was in rough shape, but it was legible, having survived in the low oxygen conditions beneath the body armor. Hashish repeated the action with each of the other dead jundie, coming up with two more legible ID cards. The writing was in Arabic, but Jeff could have one of the interpreters translate it later.

His task complete, Jeff turned his attention to the rest of the checkpoint. He walked beyond the burning Yazzes to the parking area on the left side of the road. Bits of flesh from the suicide bomber were scattered across the entire area. Jeff had to watch where he stepped to avoid getting any on his boots.

Mostly, the pieces were unidentifiable, but he was able to see three ribs, stripped of skin and charred, as if fresh from a BBQ grill. In another spot, a finger was apparent, tendons hanging from the mangled stump like pieces of dirty kite string.

Jeff saw the Master Sergeant stepping through some brush at the far side of the concrete slab, coming in from beyond the parking area. Jeff made his way over.

"Check this out, L.T.," the Master Sergeant said, holding up a severed head by singed hair in his right hand as if it were a trophy. Only the grim expression on his face separated him from a proud hunter. "Found this about twenty meters that way," he continued, motioning with his free hand. "Thing must have traveled a hundred fifty meters."

Jeff imagined the head popping off the body like a champagne cork, flying in a hundred-foot-high parabola before thunking down in the brush.

The Master Sergeant carried his prize back to the road, tossing it by the burned-out engine block. Jundie rotated in from their posts to view the bomber. Echoes of "Sudan man" were making their rounds, initial suspicions apparently confirmed by the head. Jeff didn't understand how they could determine nationality from the battered lump of fractured bone and tortured flesh, its eye holes a mass of gore and its mouth a gob of splintered teeth, but judging by the hate-filled visages and flying spittle, there was little doubt.

A few of the jundie kicked the head. Not hard enough to send it skittering back across the parking lot like a soccer ball, but hard enough to make a thumping sound, not unlike a wet drum or ripe watermelon. Puzzled by the tone, Jeff took a closer look and noticed fissures along the skull. Either the explosion or the force from landing had shattered the skull, knocking out the brains and leaving cracked bone held together by scalp. He was reminded of the shell of a hardboiled egg, fractured pieces held together after peeling by a thin inner-shell membrane.

Jeff gave the head a soft kick or two for propriety's sake, the tip of his boot touching the skull just hard enough to result in an oddly melodic thump. He barely registered the sound. He was numb.

Hashish and Simmons were busy getting the dead jundie into body bags, their faces solemn and determined. Some of the jundie saw their efforts and pitched in, laboring to force stiff limbs into the confines of black plastic bags.

Some of the jundie were shell-shocked, wandering around with a dull look in their eyes, AKs hanging slack. Strings of Arabic flew from the Iraqi officers, corralling the jundie back to the perimeter.

A door slammed. Jeff looked over to see Senior Chief Moore standing by the ambulance. It took off back toward the fort, loaded with injured jundie and civilians, a pair of Yazzes front and rear as escort. Senior made his way back toward the triage area, his eyes red-rimmed from fatigue and smoke.

"That's it, L.T.," he said, his voice flat. "I did all I could. The girl died." Senior looked down for a second, swallowed, and continued. "We've got a few more here I need to take care of, but the worst are headed back for medevac."

"You did all you could," Jeff said, not knowing what else to say. Jeff knew from experience Senior took each loss personally, a weight on his shoulders to be carried in perpetuity, each casualty adding to the burden.

"I know, but I always wonder if I could have done more," Senior replied, turning to take care of the remainder of the wounded.

Jeff walked over to where Nas and the Major were talking to Captain Ahmed, the officer in charge of the checkpoint at the time of the explosion. Ahmed's face was covered in soot and his uniform was torn from where he had been thrown to the asphalt in the initial blast.

"We can stay here with you," Jeff heard the Major say, his hand on Ahmed's shoulder.

"No, Major. No matter what happens, you must leave back to the fort. No matter what you see and hear from the jundie, you must leave. This must be left to us. We," Ahmed motioned to himself and Nas, "must prove the Iraqi Army will not bow to the terrorists. Without any help."

"I understand," the Major said, nodding. The Major solemnly surveyed the carnage. He turned to Jeff.

"All right. Let's head back." The Major raised his radio and transmitted orders to the rest of the team. No words were spoken as they walked back to the Humvees. Jeff wanted to fill the silence, but how could words describe the gruesome display they had witnessed?

The three Yazzes were still on fire, billowing black smoke, their flames hardly abated. A row of body bags were lined up along the side of the road. Families of the dead civilians would soon be coming to claim their dead relatives, a process that was becoming painfully routine.

The ambulance was back for another load. Senior Chief was loading the last of the wounded.

Jeff thought of their ride to the checkpoint, their exuberance and high spirits. It seemed like a lifetime ago. He checked his watch, the crystal face glistening yellow, reflecting brimstone particulate yet to clear from the air. Thirty minutes had passed since their arrival, maybe less.

"I'm going back in the ambulance," Senior Chief said to the Major. The Major nodded.

Jeff jumped in the Humvee seat vacated by Senior.

"This is Reaper 7. Everyone's here," the Master Sergeant's voice crackled over the radio.

"Roger, 7. Let's go," the Major replied.

The two Humvees drove off down the road.

Dear Mr. Sandman

Jason Poudrier

I'm sorry, I probably killed you,
but there is no way of knowing;
I flipped the switch two days ago.
But you probably haven't been
in that ditch long, maybe just since
you crawled there for safety when there
was no other place to crawl, like a cockroach
sprayed with Raid, never dying on
contact but just after, or maybe
you were in the road when the first
unit passed and they moved you off to the side.

I'm sorry for the flies that swarm you;
they swarm me too, they land on my food,
they land on my lips, they bite the exposed
parts of my arms and legs. At least
you don't have to worry about the
Bagdad Boils and dysentery:
I was up itching and shitting all last night.

I'm sorry for the delay of your
burial; thank you for settling
for a few thin sheets of sand that ripple
darkly over your wounds and keep me from
recognizing you. And I will not
be able to attend your ceremony,
except maybe to place your body into a bag.

Then we will be close
because I'll hold you briefly in my arms,
and I will know you forever and
see your sand-masked face often
at the mall or the grocery store
on busy days, and you'll follow me
into the liquor store and keep me company
when I'm at home alone,
and we'll each have a drink.

THE HUNGRY GHOSTS
~ Susan O'Neill ~

It is 1969. The Private and I are driving to the Kim Long Orphanage in Hue on our day off from the 22nd Surgical Hospital in Phu Bai. The Private is at the wheel of a jeep with "Phu Bai Is Alright" painted on the front. "Alright" is bad grammar, but that's the way the catchphrase has been passed down. Nobody knows who started it, or at what point in the base camp's half-dozen years of existence—or whether the nameless coiner was being sarcastic or sincere.

We are maybe five miles out of Phu Bai, and we pass a compound: shacks built of cardboard, corrugated metal and cinder block, surrounded by a chain-link fence topped with concertina wire.

Residents of this lean-to village squat on their heels in the hard-packed dust yard. Some cook over small braziers. A mother nurses her infant. A child defecates on the ground; another scratches the dirt with a stick. Silent old men watch our jeep pass.

"What is that place?" I ask the Private.

"A relocation camp, Lieutenant," he says. "Every time I come by, there's more people in there."

I ask who is relocating these people, and from where. He says it is the U.S. military; the people come from little villages in the countryside. "There's probably two reasons they're in there," he says. "One, it gets people out of the fighting."

And?

"It lets the army keep an eye on 'em. They're supposed to be friendlies, but you never know. This way, they won't get into trouble if they're not."

An old woman grips the fence, following us with spectral eyes.

Americans tend to move around. We bury our dead; if we have the time and inclination, we visit their graves. The cemetery staff clips the grass for us and removes our flowers when they wilt. Cemeteries in the U.S. are secondary to space occupied by the living. We can move away from a cemetery with a clean conscience.

In Viet Nam's countryside, families keep altars adorned with pictures of their dead ancestors. They cover these altars with food, joss sticks, paper "money." Family graves are a family responsibility; caring for an ancestor's resting place is bound with caring for the ancestor's spirit. Ancestors have been on earth before, so their spirits provide guidance. Ancestors must be honored if the living want to progress here and live well in the next life. If an ancestor is not buried properly, or honored properly after death, if he is abandoned, his "hungry ghost" might roam the earth unmoored. Perhaps, in his desperation, he might do the family ill.

It is not easy to move from one's ancestor's grave in Viet Nam. You can bring the shrine, but you must leave the bones, and this has consequences. You cannot turn the grave over to the cemetery groundskeeper; there is none. Perhaps, when you leave, the grave will be ground beneath the treads of a tank. Perhaps foreigners will set a motor pool tent over it on a military hospital compound, as we did at the 22nd Surg (Phu Bai is alright). Perhaps it will be blown apart or stained with the blood of anonymous soldiers, your soldiers or theirs. Your ancestor will not rest well without your hands tending the earth above his bones.

Hue, the Paris of Vietnam, has been owned, gambled with, and lost by many. It is watered by the Perfume River and surrounded by gentle hills. There is a college; there are French-style villas and ruins from native royalty. Young women flutter through downtown streets on bicycles and scooters, elegant butterflies in silk ao dais, those long dresses split to the waist and worn over silk trousers. Hue has rich history, poetry, refinement.

Seen from a distance, it is a jewel.

Up close, war has taken its toll.

The Citadel is Hue's old Capitol, a city within the city. It was the court of Vietnamese emperors before the French arrived. The Citadel had temples, homes, halls with inlaid ceramic thrones, grand tables, tapestries, imposing sculptures of fierce guardian lions.

The Citadel survived the country's subjugation by the Chinese, the Japanese, and the French. But not the American War's 1968 Tet Offensive.

The US military had expected peace during Tet, Viet Nam's New Year.

For days, they watched families clean house, cook, tend ancestors' altars and graves, buy fireworks. For days, unwatched, the North Vietnamese Army and the Viet Cong cleaned and assembled weapons, pored over maps, set troops in place.

On the eve of the holiday, when fireworks exploded, so did the city of Hue.

Now, a year after the smoke cleared, a year after the bodies of thousands were found, the unclaimed buried in mass graves, I stand in the Citadel's throne room. There are shell-holes in the room's vaulted ceiling. A colossal carved pillar is splintered like a bone; a grand lion smashed; a massive urn blown to rubble. The throne itself shattered. Monsoon rains will beat through the perforated roof and rot the century-old tapestries. There is a symmetry to this—that, in this land of many wars, an ancient seat of governance is crushed by new powers that would govern. But it is heartbreaking to see such old grandeur crumble under the ruthlessness of upstarts. It is sad, wasteful, ominous as the desecration of a grave.

The buildings of Kim Long orphanage are set around a dirt courtyard. Nothing green grows here. But children do. They are a bonus crop, an ever-expanding harvest.

Most of the Kim Long children are half-American. They are radiant and ragged. Many of the Vietnamese nuns who run the orphanage are old, their sun-wrinkled faces dark against their ghostly veils like walnut shells on white tablecloths. They belong to a French missionary order. Perhaps these same small, straight-backed old women tended the bastard children of French soldiers, too.

The nuns use profits from the orphanage's industry to help keep the place afloat. When an orphaned girl becomes old enough to handle looms and sewing machines, she helps make ao dais that will be worn by young women who can afford things of beauty.

Among the women who have such disposable income are Hue's whores. One might say that the nuns and the whores are united in a cyclical, mutually-beneficial business transaction: In her fine ao dai, the whore works the bars and earns money; with her money, she buys ao dais, supporting the Kim Long orphanage.

If the whore has a half-American baby, the baby might go to Kim Long—to be tended by the nuns, who are supported by the whores— and, eventually, grow up to make ao dais. Which will help the whore support herself and, therefore, the orphanage.

I apologize: this is glib, simplistic, and unfair. What is a *whore* in Viet Nam? She is a survivor, like the children at Kim Long. She, like the nuns and orphans, is working to eat in an economy where eating is not a given.

In peacetime, she might be a shopkeeper, a farmer. A seamstress. A housewife; a mother.

I doubt, really, that many babies at Kim Long belong to whores. There are many graceful, naive young women in Viet Nam who believe that the love of a knight will raise them above the misery and the disintegration of their homeland.

What would you do with a child who looks like his father when the father leaves and forgets you? When the father is the enemy of your family, neighbors, village? What would you do when you love your baby—but keeping her means that both of you will die?

You bring her to the nuns at Kim Long.

Perhaps you visit. But there is such pain in that small face, with its father's eyes.

Perhaps you stop visiting.

The children of Kim Long orphanage do not play. They squat in the dusty courtyard. Their eyes fasten on me, hungrily. They hang back; then they approach, brush fingers over the hair on my arms, reach to be hugged.

How, if you are an old woman of the Lord, do you teach a village of children to play, while you run the factory, cook the rice that keeps everyone alive, pay protection money to the ARVN and the VC, pray to your apathetic God, and keep the entire compound from being blown to bits?

Play is not a high priority.

In Kim Long orphanage, the babies sometimes die of nothing. It is not always disease that claims an infant in the long, shaded room, where so many tiny bodies lie in cribs on bare wooden slats. It is not physical starvation, because I and the Private help the nuns feed each one milk, donated by U.S. military men.

Sometimes, a baby who is too small, too weak, simply wastes away, her thin flesh stretched like paper over her bones. She dies of nothing.

Perhaps her ancestors are angry. Perhaps they are hungry for company.

Perhaps they understand this life too well, and hold out a rare and special mercy to her innocent soul.

That Saigon Night
Horace Coleman

The woman I'd rented
drug me into the shower afterwards.

I hated using that shower.
The smells it washed away
were better than those it left.

With no language but touches,
we slept with her head on my chest,
my stomach under her thigh.

More poor than whore and
more lonely than lustful,
we forgot our wars for a while:
two different browns, poured together
under the green mosquito net.

Spring in Jalula

Hugh Martin

1.

The air is exhaust smoke, desert heat, the black
sewage-streams that don't dry.

Cows graze beside the river of shit; their noses sift
through soggy trash.

2.

Last year, the liquor store was hit with two RPGs;
today, the store is a pile of brick.

When buying a car, it is cheaper to buy
the one with bullet holes.

3.

Mohammad, the ten-year old who doesn't go to school,
sells everything; when you hand him 300 dinars, he runs

through the streets, returns with Pepsi, chicken
falafel. *Zam-zam?* he asks. *DVD, freaky-freaky? Knife?*

4.

After weddings, the people fill the sky
with red tracers fired from Kalashnikovs;

the tracers pass through darkness, but somewhere
they fall back to Iraq.

5.

There is always a new bomb. Each week,
someone finds one, hidden

beneath bricks, buried beside curbs. At dusk,
people burn trash by the river. The smoke: white and blue.

6.

Daud, the town bum, walks the streets barefoot;
the cuts on his toes never heal. When he sleeps

on the same piece of cardboard beside the vendor stands,
he yells all night in broken English,

but no one ever knows what he's saying.

ONE BULLET
~ Spencer Carvalho ~

"A bullet is the quickest way to solve a problem. It's also the quickest way to start one." I'll never forget that. There's a good chance that it will be on my tombstone.

Every citizen of Brazil is required to register with the military despite the fact that the country had not had a war since fighting with the Allies in WWII. I find that impressive. All this time without a war. The only thing better than winning a war is finding a way to prevent one.

I learned about the registration process when I turned eighteen. My mom is American and my dad is Brazilian. I was born in Brazil but less than a year later my family moved to America. Because of this, I have dual citizenship, meaning that I am both an American citizen and a Brazilian citizen, an issue that didn't really have a big impact on my life until Brazil went to war.

I received a letter one day notifying me that I could join the Brazilian military because we were going to war. I had no idea what was going on. I checked the news to see if there was anything on about a war in South America. All I found was stuff about celebrity scandals. I did find some stuff online. It seemed that conflicts between Brazil and Columbia had been rising. It had gotten so bad that Brazil was now going to have its first war in decades. Actually it wasn't really with Columbia as a country. It was more a war with the drug cartels in Columbia who had recently taken over the Colombian government in a violent siege. So, yeah, Brazil was going to war with Columbia, but it was a war that many Columbian soldiers were refusing to participate in.

I didn't need to go. Since I was an American citizen, I could have stayed in America. I was in my final year at college. I had a very successful job as a professional gamer. I got paid to play video games. Everything was great. I can't explain and don't understand what came over me. For some reason I felt I had to go. I wasn't a violent guy. I was even planning on joining the Peace Corps after college. Maybe I liked the certainty of the war, a peaceful country versus ruthless drug cartels. America hadn't had a war with such moral certainty since World War II.

Before I left the country, I went to talk to some of my Brazilian family members who were also living in America. My father had died a long time ago. He was a firefighter. I went to go see my aunt, my nine-year-old cousin, and my grandpa. My little cousin wanted to go and fight but clearly was too young to understand the situation. He wanted to fight the soldiers with a "ninja sword." My grandpa used to be a cop and wanted to go, too, despite being eighty-three. He was filled with so much piss and vinegar they probably could have duct-taped a missile to his forehead and he would have head-butted the enemy.

The main reason I went to see them was to learn as much as I could about Brazilian culture. Since moving, I had only gone back to Brazil a few times. It had been nine years since my last visit. I also wanted to learn more Portuguese. Yes I know, I'm Brazilian, but can't really speak Portuguese. I could speak it when I was little but over time I forgot. To make things worse, I studied Spanish in high school. The two languages are similar, so sometimes when I try to speak one language I accidentally speak the other.

They taught me a few things about Brazil. I learned about the Amazon and about Brazilian martial arts. They updated me on what was going on with my family members still living in Brazil. They told me a lot about the country's history. My cousin gave me his English-to-Portuguese guidebook to help me learn the language.

On the plane ride down, I studied the English-to-Portuguese guidebook and filled out the paperwork to decide what areas I would train in. I decided to become a sniper because I always liked playing the sniper class in videogames. I'll repeat that, I decided to become a sniper because I always liked playing the sniper class in videogames. Yes, I know that's a stupid reason, but a lot of stupid decisions get made during wartime.

After a nine-hour plane ride, I landed in Rio de Janeiro. Rio is nice. Whenever they show footage of Brazil on TV it's usually of Rio. Oftentimes it's footage of the huge Christ the Redeemer statue that overlooks Rio. My cousin Paulo met me at the airport. He was also in the army. He was a pilot, so we didn't see each other much during training. The country wasn't prepared for a war this big, so there wasn't enough space at the training grounds. This meant that any soldier who lived driving distance from the training grounds could sleep at home and drive to and from training. Since the training ground was in Rio de Janeiro and Paulo lived there, I got to stay with Paulo, his wife, Helena, and his seven-year-old son, Junior, during my training. I had never met his wife or son before.

My first night there was a lot of fun. Paulo could speak some English so he would translate for me. Paulo told this story about how when I was five I spent the summer with my grandma and grandpa in Brazil. This was before they moved to America and way before grandma got sick and passed away. I liked to feed my grandparent's chickens, so Paulo would call me *galo*, which meant Rooster. It would make me mad, and one time it made me so mad that I head-butted him. I must have hit him really hard because he got a bloody nose. Junior thought the story was hilarious.

Paulo waited until his wife and kid went to bed and then told me a lot about what was going on. The drug cartels had violently taken over the Colombian government. Brazil spoke out the loudest about the takeover. It's believed that the war either started over Brazil's speaking out or that the cartels wanted control of the Amazon jungle, the majority of which belongs to Brazil. The smaller South American countries weren't officially taking a military stance, but unofficially they all supported us and secretly sent supplies. If South America was a family, then Brazil was the big brother who was expected to keep things under control.

Brazil's population was 193 million while Colombia's population was 43 million, so had this been a regular war it would have been an easy win for Brazil. If only. Colombia had drug money so it could afford better weapons and mercenaries. More than half of its army consisted of mercenaries. The amount of money they had from drug sales was ridiculous. Our fellow South American countries were supporting us with supplies, but the entire world was financing the cartels through drug sales. Try explaining to a junkie in the United States that they should quit buying because they were financing criminals in South America and see how well that works.

Many Colombian patriots refused to follow the cartel's rule and wanted their country back. These guys were called the Colombian Rebels and they were on our side. I was really interested in America's involvement. Pablo told me that the United Nations had imposed sanctions, which meant that it would probably get involved the day after the war ended, and the United States government declared that it wouldn't get involved in a foreign war. The fact that Colombia was hiring private U.S. military companies like Blackwater might have influenced their decision.

Training was brutal. Apparently everyone in Brazil is in great shape. In America I hadn't gotten used to all the fat people. My first week in Brazil I only saw one overweight lady. She might have been pregnant; I couldn't really tell.

I was worn out, but it wasn't just the workouts. For a peaceful country, there sure are a lot of martial artists. Mixed martial arts actually started in Brazil. Technically, mixed martial arts started a long time ago and were even a game in the early Olympics, but the sports of Mixed Martial Arts and Ultimate Fighting Championship were started in Brazil. It gained popularity through street-fighting matches and eventually became popular in America, so these people know how to fight.

They taught over thirty different types of martial arts at the training grounds. You could choose which styles you wanted to learn. I learned Jeet Kune Do, Ninjutsu, and Capoeira. This was in addition to basic training and my sniper classes. My reasons for choosing these styles were somewhat silly. I chose Jeet Kune Do because it was the martial arts style that Bruce Lee created and I think that Bruce Lee was really cool. I chose Ninjutsu because that was the fighting style of the ninja. And I chose Capoeira because Capoeira is a Brazilian martial arts style, so there were a lot of Capoeira classes. They actually teach Capoeira in schools as a gym class so there were a lot of instructors. This meant that I could fit one of the classes into a free spot in my schedule.

The sniper classes were the hardest. With basic training I could just copy everyone else. During sniper training, the instructor, Mr. Costa, would lean in close and whisper advice to us. It was clearly very important but I had no idea what he was saying. I was learning the language but there was no time for me to become fluent. I eventually got paired up with a guy named Victor. Victor was fluent in English. He would translate for me. We soon became friends.

One day when I showed up for training, I couldn't find Victor. I searched for a while and eventually found him sitting by himself under a tree, crying. He said he didn't want to kill anyone. He said that he couldn't do it. He kept talking about how he joined to make his family proud, but couldn't take a life. He worried about his soul. He said he would rather die than end a life. I was not prepared for this outpouring of emotion. I had never seen an adult man cry like that. I felt pity for him but also understood what he was talking about. He eventually became my spotter. It made sense. Snipers would often pair up with a spotter who would use a spotting scope to help them with distance, angle, and atmosphere, and since he spoke English, we were an obvious match. This way he could stay in the army and wouldn't have to kill anyone.

We were told to give ourselves call signs, nicknames. Victor chose Victory. I couldn't think of anything in time so my instructor chose a name. He called me Baby Eater. I did not like the name. I still hate that name. I can't understand why he picked such a weird call sign. Maybe it was for intimidation. Maybe he wanted to motivate the others to come up with their own call signs. He wouldn't let me change it, either.

Training was strange. I had never fired a gun before training. I had played paintball before and was really good at it, but that was my only prior experience with a gun-like weapon. The first time I fired a gun, I was shocked. I wasn't prepared for the sound. Gunfire is a lot louder in real life than in the movies. I started off terrible, but was holding my own by the end. I really didn't like my gear. My sniper rifle was too old. We used something called a Ghillie suit, which is like a camouflage blanket that goes over you to hide your position. Mine smelled like pee, probably because someone peed in it. It was the best they had to offer.

On the last day of training, the instructor walked up to me and pulled out a note card. He read something to me from that note card in English: "A bullet is the quickest way to solve a problem. It's also the quickest way to start one." During my entire time training it was the only thing he said to me that I understood. Of all the things he could have translated, he chose that. I guess he thought it was the most important thing he could teach me.

Our first mission was in the Amazon where most of the fighting took place. A Brazilian arms dealer was supplying the Colombian soldiers with weapons and maps of the Amazon. We were sent in to take out the arms dealer.

The Amazon jungle is a strange place. It covers 1.7 billion acres, which makes it the largest jungle in the world. More than half of it is in Brazil, but part of it is in Colombia. There are dangerous species like jaguars, piranhas, and vampire bats, but what really creeped me out is that there are at least sixty-seven isolated tribes. These tribes have had no contact or very little contact with the outside world. Meaning that if they saw me, then they would have no idea what I was, and we all know how people react when they encounter scary new things.

There were eight two-man teams. We were all sent on different paths to the target. Whoever got there first was to eliminate the target. Victory led the way through the jungle with his machete. We were the first ones there. The target was waiting with a supply of weapons. We found a hide site and set up our position.

I had my old sniper rifle, my sidearm, a knife, basic survival gear, and my Ghillie suit that smelled like pee. Victory had his spotting scope, a Ghillie suit that didn't smell like pee, basic survival gear, a machete, my extra ammo, and extra water. Oftentimes a spotter carries a weapon too, but since Victory didn't want to kill anyone, he carried extra water instead. The extra water might have been why we got there so much quicker than the other sniper teams.

Victory measured the range and altitude. I steadied my rifle and waited for the perfect shot. It was a long wait. I never had to wait this long while playing video games. As I waited, I thought about what I was going to do. I was going to legally murder someone. This one bullet in the chamber could end a life. It could make me a murderer and a hero. It could put me on a path that would change me forever. One bullet would end this man's life.

When the target got into position I pushed aside all my thoughts about moral consequences and whispered to myself, "One shot, one kill." I pulled the trigger and nothing. The rifle didn't fire. The old crappy rifle, which I didn't even like, didn't fire. The target was walking towards his jeep. I knew I had to hurry. I realized I still had my safety on. I turned it off and fired. I had just made my first confirmed kill. I had been thinking about how that one bullet might change my life. I was right.

They say the first kill is the hardest, and they're right. I didn't feel good about killing him. In movies and video games someone gets shot and just falls down without any blood. This was different. There was a lot of blood. I was not used to blood. I was a very peaceful person. I didn't even like to go fishing, but there I was staring at my first kill. The gore bothered me, but what bothered me more was how quickly I got over it.

After my first kill I got brand-new equipment. Since my target was a weapons dealer, I got some of the weapons we acquired from him. I got a brand-new sniper rifle with a silencer and a high-quality scope. I got a Ghillie suit that didn't smell like pee. I got a silencer for my sidearm. I got a camouflage outfit made of some kind of fabric that really handled the heat well. The guys back at the base couldn't figure out what the suit was made of. It must have been some kind of new fabric. Of all the new items, the sniper rifle was my favorite. A stinky Ghillie suit is an inconvenience, but the new sniper rifle improved my chances of survival. The best part about the new rifle was that instead of a rifle that could fire one shot and then need another bullet loaded into it, my new rifle had a clip so I could fire off multiple rounds. It also had a bipod on the front so I could steady my shots better.

Days turned into weeks which turned into months. My confirmed kills reached double digits and was rising. I was getting better at sniping. A lot better. I'm not sure why I was so good at sniping. Possibly my years of video-game playing honed my hand-eye coordination and taught me strategy. Also I was really patient. When I was a hyper, energetic little kid I could wait for hours in a hiding spot waiting for a chance to scare someone. Patience seemed to be one of the most important skills a sniper could have. The martial arts helped, too. I never got into hand-to-hand combat, but the martial arts helped me with movement. The Ninjutsu helped me with stealthy movement the most. I later found out that some of the earliest snipers were Shinobi ninja in the sixteenth century. They would fire poisoned blow guns from concealed positions.

I was getting a reputation as a skilled sniper. I was also getting used to killing people. I didn't like that. I would get troubled on occasion. I would remember that all these men were once children with mothers and that those mothers cried when they found out what had happened to their sons. Whenever I had trouble sleeping, I would remind myself that these were bad people. All the good Colombian soldiers joined the Colombian rebels and were on our side. The remaining soldiers were so weak that they would rather kill innocents than stand up to an unjust government. And the mercenaries were amoral jerks who would kill anyone for the right price. Although I was ending their lives, I was saving all the people that they would kill. What I did was necessary. I was removing evil from the world. That helped me sleep better.

During training they taught us different ways of shooting: shoot to wound, shoot to damage, and shoot to kill. When you shoot to wound, you aim for a limb, usually to slow down a squad or to lure out other victims. When you shoot to damage, you aim for the torso. This is one of the most popular ways to shoot because it's the easiest, because the torso makes the biggest target. With this type of shooting, the bullet causes so much damage that the target eventually dies. The main problem with this type of shooting is that the target sometimes lives, because if the target is wearing good enough body armor, then they're fine.

Then there is shooting to kill. This is when you aim for the head, particularly the kill point. The kill point is a part of the brain in the back of the head near the top of the neck. It's considered to be the only part of the body you can shoot and cause an instantaneous death. They don't have time to realize they are going to die. They don't even have time to feel any pain. It's a painless death. I always shot to kill. Even though they were the enemy, I didn't want to cause unnecessary pain. Plus, I always wanted to be sure that I killed my target.

I was getting better at Portuguese, too. I still couldn't speak it very well, but I could understand almost all of it. I only needed Victory to translate for me when I wanted to say something. As a sniper there weren't many times when I needed to speak.

They eventually set up a system called Info Net. It was similar to how cops use dispatch or how C.I.A. agents use handlers. Info Net was a base where all the tactics and strategies were worked out. All the major orders had to go through Info Net first. Any Brazilian soldier with a way of communicating could contact Info Net, give their security code, and get information or supply them with intelligence. We could also use them as operators to connect us with other soldiers. When it got set up, Victory received a headset so he could contact them easily. I didn't get one, but since he was my translator, it wouldn't have done me much good.

Over time I kept hearing rumors about something called The Big One. I didn't know what it was. When Victory asked Info Net what it was, he was told that it was confidential and he needed a larger security clearance. We still didn't know what the Big One was, but we knew that it was real. The rumors were that The Big One was some kind of special weapon. I found out what it was during the Battle of Rio.

The state of Rio de Janeiro is more than double the size of Hawaii and had over 15,500,000 residents. It was one of the most population-dense states in the country. That made it a good target. At that time most of the fighting had gone on in the Amazon jungle. This meant there were very few civilian casualties.

Colombian battleships were seen off the coast of Rio approaching the coastline. Brazilian battleships were already in position to protect Rio, and all the soldiers who were residents of Rio were ordered to relocate so they could defend it and help evacuate civilians. Since I trained there and was staying with Paulo, I was counted as a resident. I thought it would be a waste of time because I wasn't going to be able to help anyone evacuate.

When Victory and I got there, the battleships were engaged in combat. I knew that Helena and Junior were still somewhere in the city, but had no idea where. The battleships were out of range of my rifle and there wasn't anything I could do to help people evacuate, so I just watched the battle from the beach. What I saw during that battle changed how I think of war. The Brazilian navy was by far the most advanced of all the South American countries. They had more ships and more soldiers. For every Colombian battleship in the water there were two Brazilian battleships. It should have been a simple win.

It looked like the Brazilian navy was winning when the jets flew in. They were Colombian jets. There were fewer than fifty pilots flying fewer than fifty jets with over a billion dollars' worth of explosives. They flew in fast and dropped their bombs and within ten minutes the Brazilian battleships were destroyed. It was a battle that Colombia had won purely by having more money.

As I watched the ships sink into the ocean, I realized what was going to happen next. Their ships were going to invade the shore. This was supposed to be a simple battle. The only reason any ground troops were even called in was to help evacuate civilians and to fight just in case any of the battleships made it through to the shore. We were vastly outnumbered.

It was ominous watching the battleships slowly approach the shore, but it gave me enough time to get ready. I went into a nearby home and grabbed a pillow. Then I ran to the beach. I removed the inside of the pillow because all I really needed was the pillow case. I filled it with sand and tied off at the end. Then I found Victory, borrowed a car, and started up the mountain. By the time we reached the Christ the Redeemer statue, the battleships were pretty close to the shore. From the statue you could see the shore and a lot of the city below. I set the sandbag near the edge of the statue and used it to steady my rifle. Victory realized what I was doing and gave me a look that I will never forget. I don't know what he was thinking, but I assume that he was contemplating the moral ramifications of using a Christ statue as a sniper point. He looked at the statue for a few seconds and then looked down at the city below. There were still a lot of people in the city. I'm not sure what went through his mind, but he set up his spotting scope without my needing to convince him of anything.

It was close to dusk when the battleships reached the shore. When the soldiers emerged, I could see that they were mainly mercenaries. You could always tell the difference by the uniforms. They shot at everything that moved. Maybe they got paid per kill or maybe they just wanted to kill. I've often wondered about the type of person who chooses a job where they kill for profit. I was fighting for free.

The light was gone by the time they were in range—which was perfect. I destroyed all the lights that shone on the statue at night. I didn't want anyone to see where we were. The streetlights showed me where they were. I aimed for the leaders. You could usually tell who they were because they were the ones yelling at the other soldiers. I wanted to slow them down so I could give the civilians a chance to escape and provide time for reinforcements.

I shot for hours. It was the perfect sniper point. With my silencer they couldn't hear me and they couldn't see me, so I never had to relocate to a new position. I lost track of how many I killed. As morning approached, the reinforcements arrived. I continued shooting and only stopped when I ran out of bullets. With the exception of my sidearm, I had used every single bullet I had. I even used up all the spare ammo Victory carried. Before the Battle of Rio, I had 33 confirmed kills. I asked Victory how many kills I made that night. It took him a while to answer. Maybe he thought it would be better if I didn't know or maybe he wanted some time to double-check the numbers. I grew impatient, so I asked him again, and he told me. Ninety-one confirmed kills. The U.S. record for confirmed sniper kills was 109. My new total was 124.

When the light came we could clearly see the city below. Bodies were everywhere. Soldiers and civilians were intermingled. I wasn't sure how many lives I saved but I could see how many I failed to save. Victory walked to the foot of the statue and said a prayer. I just stared in shocked horror at all the bodies. This was a massacre.

Before Victory could finish praying, we got a call from Info Net. He put his head near mine so I could hear the message, too. It was a message sent out to all the soldiers in Rio. They finally told us what the Big One was. The Big One was a missile, a very big missile, an old Soviet missile. It was aboard a jet that was headed our way. It would be at our location within two minutes. We had jets in the air to stop it but if the missile was released, then the explosion would be so big that it would probably kill most of the survivors from the Battle of Rio. We were informed that the jet carrying the Big One was a high-altitude jet, so if the missile was released we would have some time before it hit the ground to take cover. But if it was released, it couldn't be stopped. The missile had an anti-targeting system that would derail any missiles fired at it. It also had a bulletproof protective casing. If we had Predator drones in the area, we could manually fly one into the missile. But we weren't prepared for this, so none were available. The message ended, and Victory continued praying.

I looked at the mountain I was on. If the missile were released, it would probably get released inland to do the most damage. We could go down the side of the mountain facing the Atlantic Ocean and the mountain would act as a giant shield. It wasn't a great plan but I was improvising.

Victory stopped praying and looked at me. He told me that the Big One had been released. I looked up at the sky but I couldn't see anything. I slung my rifle over my shoulder, grabbed Victory, and ran. Victory was running beside me when he grabbed my shoulder and stopped. He didn't say a word, just took off his headset and handed it to me. I put it on.

"Hello?" I asked.

"Promise me you'll take care of Helena and Junior," said Paulo.

"Of course but...."

I then realized what was happening, and looked up. I watched Paulo crash his jet into the missile. Fire filled the sky. I later found out that if the missile had hit the ground, his family would have been in the blast radius along with thousands of others. He had saved thousands of lives. He was a hero. To sacrifice one's life for the greater good is one of the noblest acts a human being can commit.

The next day I went to my training grounds. I found my sniper teacher and told him that I wanted to change my call sign. I explained in Portuguese all that I had been through. I told him about the Battle of Rio. He agreed to let me change it. I was no longer known as Baby Eater. From that point on I was known as Rooster.

A lot of people attended Paulo's funeral. There were the people he saved and their families, but also fellow soldiers. There wasn't a body to bury so they buried his medals instead. I had also received medals for my involvement in the Battle of Rio but couldn't help feeling that he deserved them more. They placed a memorial over his grave.

Later, I made sure that Helena and Junior took a plane to America and were granted American citizenship. They stayed with my aunt, grandpa, and cousin. I promised Paulo I would take care of them and wasn't going to break that promise for anything. I wasn't able to join them in America, though. I couldn't leave the war until it was over. There was still much left to do.

After I returned to duty, Victory asked me what was next. I told him that the world record for most confirmed sniper kills was 505. I had a new goal. When Paulo died, something in me died too. I no longer had compassion for the enemy. With every new kill, I became a better soldier, but lost more of my humanity.

I fear that this war is going to turn me into something I don't like. But until this war ends, I'll continue fighting. I'll keep trying to survive. No one has managed to kill me yet.

A Photograph of Zapata

Perry Higman

I cleaned up the walls
of my office today.
It was time
for a change.
I gave away an Audubon print
of a redwing blackbird,
threw out a poster of Einstein,
and took down
cluttered quotes
from Sophocles, Shakespeare,
Borges, Montaigne
and Frost.
I don't need to proclaim my being
through them right now.

But I am keeping
the picture postcard
of Emiliano Zapata
sitting next to
Pancho Villa
in the gilded chairs
in President Carranza's office,
whom they had just run out
of Mexico City . . .

      A crowd of men breathing
      warm tequila air

            in the president's office

      The weight of wide hats,
      matted black hair

            in the president's office

      Hands used to holding
      pistols and reins

in the president's office

Perfumed silk suits
mixed with bullets and spurs

in the president's office

and Zapata's eyes,
obsidian eyes,
cat eyes prowling
the Morelos canefields,
eyes that still terrify and freeze
those who nervously
shuffle through papers
and plans

in the president's office.

Beirut Pastoral

Don Schofield

When a man hath taken a new wife
he shall not go out to war...
but shall remain at home for one year....

—Deuteronomy 24:5

All day the guns pound from the mountains.
When a shell hits the arbor shakes.
The sandbags fall unless we prop them up.
Here in Besaam's garden
my new father-in-law talks
of mists in the Bekaa Valley,
deep grass hiding the ruins.
Dust hangs in the failing light. Before eight
we go home past the searchlights.

And his words go with us through the rubble—
to be a weed in Baalbek, a stone piled
in that Roman library with field and sheep.
The Romans left that valley bitter, defeated,
to shepherds who now sit and smoke and follow
the trails of jets across the dusk sky.

Home is harsh lights, locked doors,
torn shutters, one room looking out
on an alley of burnt cars. My bride and I
leave our clothes behind the door and go into
that empty room. When the spotlights pass,
our bodies shine like toppled statues.

Osama's Last Porno Film
~ Henry F. Tonn ~

*Reuters revealed that an "extensive" collection of
pornographic material was found among
Osama bin Laden's effects by Navy Seals.*

Osama bin Laden was engrossed in his favorite pornographic film—a beautiful blonde with swaying bosoms administering an enthusiastic blow job to a well-endowed young man—when he heard firecrackers going off near his bedroom. His brow creased. These Pakistani children are becoming more like Americans every day, he thought. Where are their parents?

He was pondering which of his three wives would be willing to imitate the blonde porn star's ministrations when the fireworks exploded even nearer to his room. This was most peculiar. Had one of the twenty-three children in the compound got hold of something expressly forbidden? They shouldn't be attracting unwanted attention to the house.

He returned to the blonde's bobbing head.

Suddenly, a violent explosion occurred right down the hallway, followed by gunfire.

A thousand plagues, Osama thought. People are always interrupting me when I'm really busy.

He put the remote on freeze and wandered into the hallway to investigate the disturbance.

THE LAST CIVILIZED BATTLE
~ Louis M. Prince ~

In 1938 my grandmother gave me five hundred dollars for my eighteenth birthday to make a summer trip abroad. Happily, a student who sat next to me in French class suggested I join him for a free-lance bicycle trip across France. It seemed like a perfect idea. My parents were great Francophiles and had friends living in Paris and in the Midi, but instead of mooching off them, we stayed overnight for free in barns of hospitable farmers, who often gave us free meals as well.

We met lots of French cyclers on our casual journey. I have particularly fond memories of two older women (age twenty-two or so) we met along the way who preferred oral sex to intercourse because it eliminated pregnancy issues. This, in my opinion, was a very civilized attitude. I returned to the States three weeks later with $2.97 in my pocket and a lasting love of France and French culture.

Two years later when the country fell to the Nazis, I shared the deep grief of people all over the world.

I had always loved horses and horseback riding. In my college freshman year, I signed up for Artillery ROTC because their weapons were horse-drawn French 75 mm guns, 1897 models, left over from World War I. In June 1941, upon graduating with a B.A. in French Literature, I was commissioned a Field Artillery Second Lieutenant. Shortly thereafter, I found myself at Fort Bragg, N.C., in "B" Battery of the 60th Field Artillery Battalion, an integral infantry support unit of the 9th Infantry Division. We had the same old French 75s, but truck-drawn now, and I became "Battery Executive,"the man who directs the fire at the Gun Position. It was like heaven; I loved everything about the job: the mathematics, the teamwork, the smell of gunsmoke, and the roar of the guns. I could have been a Battery Executive for decades, the oldest lieutenant ever.

At that point in World War II, Allied victories were few and far between, especially in the European theater. Russia was demanding Allied ground action in Western Europe to divert some of the Nazi strength away from the Eastern Front. England and the United States were not ready for a cross-channel attack, so they compromised by attacking the western half of North Africa called the *Maghreb* by the French, who occupied Algeria and most of Morocco. Theoretically, such an attack would draw Nazi troops from Europe to defend the rear of General Rommel's forces which were driving General Montgomery's British Army ever eastward toward the Suez Canal. Resistance to our landings was expected because the French troops were commanded by General Nogues, a supporter of the Vichy Government, a puppet state of Nazi Germany in the south of France.

The landing, which was supposed to be a surprise, was not. President Roosevelt made a radio speech intended to be given simultaneous with our storming the beachhead, but high seas and submarines delayed our progress, and the Great Assault took place six hours later instead. The French were ready. Two brilliantly lighted French freighters bound northward steamed gingerly through the middle of our blacked-out convoy and radioed our presence. The French artillery regiment had already surveyed all targets on the beach and were fully prepared to fire at us day or night. No doubt the French officers toasted their good fortune with *du vin*, and waited eagerly for the coming engagement.

It was dark and the sea was rough as we reached our debarking site; everyone knew our troops would have difficulty climbing down the nets and jumping into the ramp boats. Our howitzers were unloaded by crane into the same ramp boats, but only with extraordinary effort did we manage to manhandle the guns through chest-high water and heavy surf to the beach. Shells from enemy artillery burst among scurrying riflemen, and casualties were high from gunfire and the inevitable drownings in unexpectedly high surf.

Once we were strafed by American planes given to the French under the lend-lease program before the fall of France in 1940. In war are many ironies, but to us this was extreme.

Daylight arrived and our infantry advanced, suffering more casualties from enemy ground fire. Forward Observer Ralph Williams was captured and taken directly to Meknes by train where he was wined and dined by French officers in a luxury hotel. I knew his wife and two children at home, so he never told me what else he did there. He was gone for three days.

On the third day of the battle, the Infantry Colonel in command of the 60th Infantry visited our gun position. He suddenly spied what he thought were enemy tanks approaching our right flank and peremptorily shouted orders for one of *my* howitzers to fire on them. Before his order could be executed, I saw and recognized the tanks as friendly, from our 9th Recon Troop, with prominent white stars painted on their sides. Although still a mere first lieutenant, I promptly countermanded the colonel's order, and not calmly, either. The man went hysterical, and I wondered how he ever became a regimental commander. His infantry, however, though suffering a regrettable number of casualties, accomplished their mission.

After three days the battles ended all over Morocco and Algeria with a signed truce in Algiers. On the whole, I was impressed with how well everyone in the 60th Combat Team responded to our first call to action. The French defenders had given us a gentle baptism in preparation for what was to come. In the meantime, the British had beaten Rommel at El Alamein, a victory hailed as one of the War's turning points. Tunisia would be our next battle site.

Almost immediately after the truce, the French artillery officers who had been firing on us invited us to a banquet at their headquarters just outside of Port Lyautey. There were about ten of us and about twenty of them. I sat next to our colonel as interpreter until the "champagne," ersatz because of the war, did me in. We ate snails, couscous, and stuffed quince while the Senegalese band, dressed in flowing white trousers and cerulean blue jackets, played the "Marseillaise" and "America the Beautiful," which they seemed to think was our national anthem.

During the meal our colonel noticed a black officer sitting by himself at a small table in the rear. When he asked why, the French colonel informed him that they were concerned some of our officers from the southern part of the United States would be offended to sit next to him. Our colonel, who was from Alabama, protested vehemently, and had a chair and place setting inserted between him and me. The dark-skinned officer spoke little English, but we all enjoyed each other's company for the rest of the evening.

Later I was detailed to teach the French officers how to use the 105 howitzer with which they were to be re-equipped in order to fight the Nazis. The French officers, all older career army men, teased me unmercifully about my accent and vocabulary. One day they supposedly taught me to say *bonjour* in Arabic so I could impress their dignified old colonel who visited my class every day. I used my "new word" and watched his jaw drop. He glared at me for a moment, then, figuring out what had happened, began to laugh. Later I learned they had actually taught me to say, "Go fuck yourself."

Afterward, there were no hard feelings, and I kept contact with some of these officers by mail for many years.

Only the officers and some non-commissioned officers in this force were actually French. Most of the troops were Arabs and Senegalese. We Americans had over 650 casualties in Morocco and the opposition suffered many more. It was indeed a waste, but it could have been worse. There was very little publicity about this engagement because it had no propaganda value. The battle, however, was a portent of experiences awaiting us.

Our 9th Infantry Division subsequently fought in Tunisia, Sicily, Normandy, Northern France, Belgium, and Germany. It was one of four divisions with over 20,000 casualties in the European War. I am proud to have been a member of it, but still grieve for the many who did not survive.

Gunpoint

Jason Poudrier

If you're holding a 50 cal.
Aimed at an Arab,
He'll do anything:
Spin around repeatedly,
Flap his arms like a
Stepped-on lizard.

He'll lift up his Arab dress
And moon you, then turn
Around and show you the front.

You didn't ask
Him to do those things:
Just turn around once with
His arms up before
Coming closer, but

There was a failure
In communication,
So as you watch
And laugh,
The 50 cal. nods
In annoyance.

After some
More squabbling and banter,
He comes forward and
Hands you a note bearing
Your BC's signature saying
He's allowed entrance into camp.
Mr. 50 cal. will have to wait.

BENZEDRINE
~ Nels Hanson ~

When they flew the fire raids over Japan, they'd take one tablet over Iwo, then another halfway between Iwo and the target.

Then one more Benzedrine coming off the target. Tonys and Zeros picked them up approaching the run, fired briefly, and were gone.

It was eight hours back to Tinian, so when they landed they'd been up 16 hours. Sometimes they'd have to go again the next night.

Two-thirds of the crews had gone down. In Lakeland's Quonset there had been eight crews. The Yale crew used to sing their fight song. They lasted two missions.

Now Lakeland's was the last crew left. Like everyone else, Lakeland remembered that when they cleared the coast and started back across the water toward home.

Lakeland was Central Fire Control Gunner, handling two top turrets by remote from his Plexiglas bubble. He had the best view of anyone on the plane.

Really, he was too tall for central fire control, and the top of his head bumped the roof of the bubble. But the doctor had passed him on.

Lakeland wanted to fly and would have been a fighter pilot if his mother hadn't refused to sign the papers. He'd worked on his father, but his mother won out.

This was much worse than flying a fighter would have been.

They had just bombed Kobe, flying pathfinder, dropping incendiaries along the docks for the formations behind them. You were in front so you didn't see if any planes went down. You never knew until you got back.

Over the intercom Fredericks had said, "They got Willy and them." Breeden was on that crew.

Once Lakeland and Breeden had got drunk together on some native cane liquor. Breeden was from a farm, too, not California, but North Carolina—tobacco. When he'd do his chores, a Negro girl would follow him around.

"What you want?" Breeden would ask. She wouldn't answer, she'd just look at him.

"Leave me alone, don't be following me," Breeden told her.

But every day she was there. Her name was Irene. She'd bring Breeden feathers, flowers, shiny stones.

"You know," Breeden said, "after a while, I got to liking her."

Breeden took her swimming one night in the river. After that, they went almost every night. He didn't go with his white girlfriend anymore. People began to talk, but Breeden didn't care.

Then Irene got pregnant and she went up North to live with a relative. Breeden never saw her again, just a picture she sent him of her and the baby. Breeden said if he made it back he was going to find her and marry her.

"He's my son," he wept.

Lakeland heard the engines thrumming in the 29's wing. The wing was silver and the moonlight shone into the bubble. The moon made a silver path across the water. He could see the waves.

The two waist gunners were asleep; Lakeland could hear their snores echoing in the tunnel.

Fredericks warned them about it, after the Nagoya raid. Everyone fell asleep from the Benzedrine. Fredericks woke up and the 29 was on autopilot, tanks low, 300 miles off the China coast.

They dropped the flak jackets and all the guns into the sea. When they landed, Fredericks had Lakeland climb up on the wing and dip a stick into the tank.

Just the tip of the stick was wet with gas.

Bridges, the tail gunner, was always asleep.

He'd almost got them killed when they'd mined the harbor at Yokohama. Bridges was airsick and left his guns, flopped down in the crawl space.

Then tonight, when the Zero jumped them and Lakeland couldn't reach it, an inch short, the rear turret's twin guns hit the stop that kept them from shooting the tail. Bridges sat there, frozen, Lakeland yelling at him through the intercom as the Zero's guns raked the stabilizer, metal flying off.

"Bridges!"

At 50 yards Bridges opened up, and the Zero exploded.

Quaid was an addict. He'd been into the morphine in the kit. Everybody knew it.

Ansard, Lavelle, Handy—all of them had something badly wrong.

But Fredericks was all right. He knew how to fly, even if he was always volunteering them for something.

The 29 was the most beautiful plane in the world. It was streamlined, like a bullet. The perfect beat of the engines made a song with words Lakeland could almost make out. The quiet vibration ran through the wing to the fuselage, into his seat, into his bones.

The singing was in his bones. It made him sleepy.

I'm sleepy, Lakeland thought, badly wrong.

His head fell back against the sheepskin of his flight jacket.

Lakeland was a kid again: his father and mother and his little sister were getting ready to go to the coast. They were excited—they hardly ever went.

His father was telling him not to try to ride the wild roan, to do his chores, milk the cows, all his regular work, but not get anywhere near the horse. When his father got back, they would load the roan in the trailer and take it over to Traver where the rodeo buyers would set up the temporary corrals.

A horse that mean would bring a lot of money.

His father and mother and his sister got into the car. He watched the old Dodge go down the drive, his mother waving from the window, holding his sister on her lap.

Then he turned and walked over to the corral.

The roan was mean, all right. He knew it would take some time. He went over to the plum tree and picked some sweet blue plums.

At first, the horse tried to bite him. Then it was eating out of his hand. The horse let him touch its neck, then between its ears.

He got into the corral with it.

"Easy, boy," he whispered.

The horse was a lot taller than he was. He ran his hand along its back. Then he turned and took the blanket from the fence. He eased it on. The roan didn't buck, just looked forward.

He got a milk stool and stood on it. Now his head was even with the roan's, almost.

Stroking the horse's back, he climbed on.

The horse stood still. He touched the roan's flanks. It began to move jerkily around the corral.

He brought the roan plums every day for two weeks.

The third day, with hardly any trouble, he got the saddle on. The fourth day he slipped on the bridle.

He sort of wished his family wouldn't come back because the roan was the best horse he'd ever had. He also liked cooking for himself, sitting alone at night in the living room, reading or listening to the radio.

He knew he couldn't keep the horse and he couldn't tell his father he had ridden it. They sent him a couple of postcards from the coast. His father had caught a big fish off the pier. His sister had gone wading. His mother sent her love.

He got up extra early the morning they were coming back. He milked the cows, swept out the barn, hosed down the driveway, got everything shipshape.

He stood by the corral looking at the roan.

He figured he had time for one more ride, but only bareback. There wasn't time for the saddle; sometimes his father left for places at three in the morning. He got on and rode around in a circle, keeping his eye peeled across the pasture to the road.

Then he saw dust moving in the distance. It wasn't his father's car, then it was. He lay flat against the horse's back and slid down. He brushed off his clothes and slipped through the gate, the roan trying to follow at his heels.

"Did it go all right?" his father asked, getting out of the car. "Everything okay?"

"Yes," he said.

"Good boy."

His mother got out and hugged him. "We missed you," she said. "Didn't we, Lorie?"

At dinner his father said, "Tomorrow we'll go to Traver. I think we can sell the roan, maybe pick up some buyers for later in the summer."

The next morning it took his father two hours to get the roan into the trailer. The horse reared, kicked, ran straight at his father. Finally, his father ran it in a circle, faster and faster, until the horse was dizzy. Then his father tied on the blindfold.

When they got the roan up the ramp, it kicked, breaking three of the trailer's wooden slats. All the way to Traver they could feel the trailer sway as the horse tried to get out.

They pulled into the bare alkali field where the corrals had been set up. Cars were parked around. It was the off-season and the rodeo stars were touring with the rodeo sponsors and buyers, testing out horses and bulls.

His father went over and talked to a man he knew. The man came back and looked through the broken trailer slats at the roan.

"Where'd you get him?" asked the man. "He's the devil himself."

His father got the horse out of the trailer and it went wild again. Two men came over and roped it around the neck. They spread out in a triangle, yanking the roan over to one of the chutes.

The blindfold had fallen off and it didn't want to go in. Then it was in but didn't want to stay. It took a long time to get the saddle on.

He and his father sat on top of the fence. A cowboy with a silk shirt, pearl buttons, a big black hat, alligator boots, walked bowlegged over to them. He was big but could hardly walk.

"Dusty Bryson," he said, lifting his hand to shake. "That your horse?"

His father nodded.

"Pretty mean, huh?"

"I'd say so."

Bryson smiled. He had a gold tooth.

"Well," he said, "we'll see. Sonny, you mind holding my watch?"

From his pocket, Bryson took out a gold watch the size of a small saucer and handed it to him. It had a chain. It was heavy gold, with swirls, guns, and spurs.

"George 'Dusty' Bryson, National Bronc Riding Champion, Madison Square Garden, 1932," the engraving said.

Bryson walked back to the stall.

"Watch this," said his father.

The roan was moving back and forth, shaking the sides of the chute. Bryson climbed up, started to get on. Three men had to hold the horse's head. Bryson swung his leg over, wound the rope around his glove. He nodded and the gate opened.

The roan threw him six feet in the air, circled the ring, and came back at him. Bryson barely made it over the fence. The horse ran into the fence, trying to get him.

"Get him in there again!" Bryson yelled. "I'll ride that son of a bitch."

Each time it took a while to get the roan back into the chute. No one wanted to get close to it. Bryson tried two, three, four times. The last time he was slow to get up.

"That's enough," said a man in a suit. "No more. Who owns this horse?" Someone pointed. He walked over to them.

"That your horse?"

His father nodded.

"Here's $200. That enough?"

"Yep."

"He's mean, all right," the man said, "awfully mean." He reached for Bryson's watch.

Now the men were trying to get the roan into a shiny metal trailer like a house trailer. It was silver and had a porthole. The horse reared and kicked and they couldn't get it to go in.

"Let's go," said Lakeland's father.

On the way back, when his father wasn't looking, he'd look back at the empty trailer. He thought he heard the roan inside it, but when he looked it wasn't there.

"Dad?"

His father watched the road.

"You know, when you were gone?"

His father nodded.

"I rode that horse."

His father didn't turn to look at him. He looked straight ahead at the road.

"I know you did, son. Just don't tell your mother."

That was all his father ever said about it.

They went home and had an early dinner and his mother was

happy about the money. She counted it, then put it in the jar in the cupboard. She asked him what he had done while they were gone.

"Nothing," he said.

He went out to the cabin by the barn. The house had only two bedrooms, so when his sister was born he had moved out there.

He liked it better in the cabin, next to the horses. He lay down and went to sleep.

But he kept hearing something like hooves kicking the cabin wall that bordered the corral. He thought it was just a dream. The roan wasn't back, it hadn't escaped.

But he heard it kicking, harder, harder. It would break down the cabin: harder, harder, waking him up . . . .

Lakeland opened his eyes. He wasn't in the cabin. He was in the ship. The ship was shaking.

Out the bubble he saw fire coming from the No. 3 exhaust manifold. He got on the intercom: "Captain, 3's going."

That's not like Fredericks, he thought, to let it get that way. It would tear the plane apart, explode the gas line.

No answer from the cockpit.

"Charlie?" he called down from the bubble. "Handy?"

He climbed down.

They were all laid out asleep. Lavelle, the belly gunner, was asleep on the floor below the mouth of the tunnel.

Now the plane was really shaking, the engine's bearings going. Any second it would catch fire.

He crawled past the gunners in the tunnel.

Up front everybody was asleep: navigator, radio operator, engineer, both pilots asleep in their seats. He shook Fredericks's shoulder.

"Fredericks!"

Fredericks slept with his mouth open. He didn't wake up. The No. 3 tachometer was varying awfully badly.

Lakeland pulled back the No. 3 throttle and upped 1, 2, and 4 by 200 rpm to 2,050.

He leaned over Derry at the engineer's panel and went through the feathering procedure, transferring all the gas from No. 3 into the other engines.

Then he turned back and upped the rpm to 2,300.

He trimmed the ship.

Lakeland pulled Fredericks from the seat, laid him down, then got in himself.

The plane was quiet. In front and below he could see Watkins, the bombardier, sleeping. He thought of Bridges asleep in the tail.

He started to go on the intercom, then stopped.

He sat still, admiring the secret lights of the dials that threw a green glow. He listened to the three remaining engines, feeling them through the wheel. The ship felt good in his hands.

Out the cockpit he could see the moon and stars, and below them the sea. He could see the Pole Star and the Southern Cross; he could go by them.

He flew the silver plane across the Pacific, toward Tinian, alone, under the moon, above the water. He'd get them home.

With everybody asleep, time stretched out.

He listened to the singing of the engines again. He wasn't sleepy anymore.

If he had the gas, he could get them all to the States, land back east somewhere. He'd find Irene, Breeden's girl, tell her what Breeden had said before he died.

But after a while he began to feel sad.

It would be the same as the roan he couldn't keep. By and by Fredericks would wake up and want to take over.

Lakeland would have to crawl back down the tunnel to his turrets.

Down to the Sea

Cynthia Ris

Those assigned to the USS Arizona at the time of the attack on Pearl Harbor are eligible for interment in the hull of the ship.

Master-at-arms calls—
0430 arrives early
the morning after shore leave.
Men won't wait for breakfast
and dough for biscuits
takes time to roll, even when
those galley slaves roll with me.
Head cook means mixing
and scrambling and frying
while the line moves by.
But I stop to dish it out while they
rib me about everything: the eggs
are runny, the gravy lumpy.
Christ! Wadduya trying to do here,
kill us? Is this horsemeat?
The horse died years ago!

It's strange, how different hands are. Sometimes
long, thin fingers—a woman's almost—belong
to the roughest voice. I get to know faces, too.
It takes longer glancing up from ladling chow,
but I mold images over time. I see them, still in line,
their faces white with ash. Eyebrows gone. Hair
singed and wiry. Shorts and shirts melted on burned flesh.
Still walking though, like later, on the quarterdeck.
The ones I saw when Captain called *Abandon Ship!*

Other times I see only what I heard—like afterwards
when Navy divers searched for live missiles
in the sunken hull, felt someone there, saw floating bodies
filling the overhead, uniforms bulging with rotted flesh,
stumps of finger bones picked clean by scavenger crabs.
I see these men too, walking by in line. . . .

Usually ship's steward
fed the officers, but once,
with the press on board,
the Admiral walked the line
like all the rest,
said he liked my pies:
the picture shows me,
head down, dishing it out,
him staring ahead. . . .

They say that at the first attack
he ran on deck, half-dressed,
pushed aside a gunner already dead.
One minute, he was there,
firing at the rising suns, the next,
the deck was blown apart. A shell
hit the forward magazine.
Most of those still on board
went with the Admiral.

The families wanted their sons back, tried
exhuming the bodies. But when body parts
came floating up and floating up, the rescue teams
bagged what they could and left the rest. The divers,
sick by now, got their wish—the men would stay.

My daughter says it's like I never left the ship.
The least I could do, she says, is stay here
when I die—a nice green field where grandkids
can come, leave flowers on my grave.

After early grub, I hit the hay—
let the galley slaves cover
the last breakfast call.
But General Quarters sounded—
battle stations. The men
already filled the magazine.

They yelled to close the hatch,
man the broadside guns.
The ladder up was slick with oil
and blood. A gunner hung
from a pole. Another seaman,
still alive, wandered past with flesh
in streamers waving from his arms.
I led him down to sick bay.
An electrician's mate, both legs gone,
lay twisted in a pool of blood. I knew
him from the striped shirt melted on
his chest. I struggled to the mainmast:
down and aft they walked in lines,
crossing the quarterdeck, eyes ahead,
flesh gone or black or ashen.
I edged past, saw the plank from ship
to quay snap and fall. Bombers swept
across again. I found myself
in the drink—oil inches thick,
fire advancing, bullets strafing the surface.
I didn't know I'd been hit till
hands were grabbing,
pulling me aboard.

At home, I watch the tape—the 50th Anniversary.
Me and my buddies, we each got to say what we
remembered. Most of us cried. We ate on board
a Navy ship. We walked the line; the sailors
dished out the food and saluted us, each one of us.

When I dogged the hatch
I might have saved some lives.
Those inside took the brunt,
but sparks and flames stayed contained.
I took the sailor to sick bay.
He might have made it up.
And that morning, I'd fed them
breakfast, each one of them.

I signed the papers. They'll play taps.
My wife will get a flag that's raised above the ship.
A diver will take me out, the sealed urn will drop—
the last reunion.

I still see them walking
early breakfast line.
None of us knew.
Only in my dreams
are they burned and dying.
That's when I match
finger bones to voices.
Always the voices—
Hey, what is this crap?
You call that pie?

Veterans
Nicholas Samaras

Back in the world, there are
bonds tighter than marriage.

Entrenched men have shared
a curious passion and forty years

and twenty years will not dispel
the musk of such intimacy.

In the beginning, the repetitive armistices grow
circles of reunions. In the interim, lives are worked,

survival fattening men who come together to honour
what no one appreciates who was not there.

Some shout across
the convention room, trying to decipher

the slender boy-faces
in their aged G.I. friends.

Absent-mindedly touching their scars,
some talk quietly of how their hands

felt to curve around a blunt instrument.
Though their hands have been empty for years,

their lives have never since
been so full or pure.

Some repeat these stories for decades
and you cannot ask them to stop. It isn't obscene to them.

It is their lives, and what they hold between them.
In the end, all war stories are love stories.

CONTRIBUTORS' NOTES

KRIS AGUILAR is a vendor of alcoholic beverages and firearms. She rides motorcycles and writes as therapy. Her husband was diagnosed with Post Traumatic Stress Disorder in 2011 and they continue to live together in Northwest Indiana.

MAROULA BLADES is an Afro-British poet/writer living in Berlin. *Domestic Cherry, Trespass Magazine, Word with Jam, The Latin Heritage Foundation, Caribbean Writer,* and *Peepal Tree* have published her work. Maroula's first poetry/music single "Meta Stasis," released by Havavision Records (U.K.) on Feb. 4, 2012, is now available as a download from iTunes.

KIRK BARRETT has produced award-winning poetry, fiction, and academic writing concerning Yugoslavia and is currently doing graduate work in Literary and Cultural Studies at Carnegie-Mellon University. He does not consider the myth of Icarus to be a fable warning about the dangers of hubris in flying too high, but rather a story depicting the need to build better wings.

BYRON BARTON spent six years in the USAR while working on a PhD in biology. After a tour in Iraq as an AST embedded with the 1/1/3rd IA Division, he completed his doctorate and began a career in academia. He is currently a professor at a Caribbean medical school.

SPENCER CARVALHO has written for various literary magazines and anthologies. His story "One Bullet" was previously published by labelmelatin.com. For other work, he invites you to Google his name.

HORACE COLEMAN was born in Ohio, lives in California, and has published in such anthologies as *Carrying the Darkness, From Both Sides Now, Men of our Times,* and *Demilitarized Zones.* His articles and poems have been published in *The Veteran, American Poetry Review, Asheville Poetry Review, Atlantic Pacific Press,* and *Callaloo.*

BRANDON COURTNEY was born and raised in Iowa and spent four years in the United States Navy. His poetry is forthcoming or appears in *Best New Poets 2009, The Journal, The Raleigh Review, 32 Poems,* and *The Los Angeles Review*, among others, and has twice been nominated for a Pushcart Prize. He recently received an Academy of American Poets award.

RICHARD DAUGHTRY was a Tech Sergeant in the United States Air Force from 1942 until September, 1945. After the war, he worked in several retail businesses until age sixty-five when he opened a used bookstore. He sold the bookstore at age eighty-seven and now lives in comfortable retirement with his wife, Lucy.

LARRY DISHON completed one tour of duty in Vietnam as an Infantry Radio Telephone Operator (RTO), for the United States Army. He received several decorations, including the Bronze Star for service to his country. This is his first publication.

LIZ DOLAN is a five-time Pushcart Prize nominee who has won an established artist fellowship from the Delaware Division of the Arts. Her second poetry manuscript, *A Secret of Long Life*, which is seeking a publisher, was nominated for the Robert McGovern Prize. Her first poetry collection, *They Abide*, was recently published by March Street Press.

NELS HANSON lives with his wife, Vicki, on the Central Coast of California. He graduated from U.C. Santa Cruz and the University of Montana, and has worked as a farmer, teacher, and contract writer/editor. His fiction received the San Francisco Foundation's James D. Phelan Award, and his stories have appeared in the *Antioch Review, Texas Review, Black Warrior Review, Southeast Review, Montreal Review,* and other journals.

PERRY HIGMAN lived in Mexico. He taught Spanish, Creative Writing, and English at Eastern Washington University for thirty-eight years and now remains very active as a climber and backcountry skier in the mountains of the Americas.

FRANK HOLLAND was born in Indiana and served in the Army from 1944 to 1946. He was stationed in the Philippines and in occupied Japan. Subsequently, he attended Indiana University and Notre Dame, and now lives in New York City. He has published over thirty short stories in the *MacGuffin, Oyez Review, Pleiades, Cicada,* the *Kit-Cat Review*, and others.

DANNY JOHNSON is a USAF and Vietnam Vet and a recipient of the Distinguished Flying Cross for combat actions in Vietnam. He is a writer of Southern fiction and has been published in many journals and anthologies, including *The Sheepshead Review, Main Street Rag Best of Raleigh Reading Series*, and *Milspeak Books*. He was nominated for a Pushcart Prize in 2011.

MONTY JOYNES lives with his wife in Boone, North Carolina, where he writes novels, nonfiction books, screenplays, and classical music libretti. Visit his website at www.montyjoynes.com.

DIANE JUDGE lives in Durham, North Carolina. She is a member of the North Carolina Poetry Society as well as the Carolina African American Writers' Collective. Her work has been published in *Black Magnolias Literary Journal, 34th Parallel, Obsidian: Literature in the African Diaspora, Frogpond,* and *Poetry South.*

"MIKE" LYTHGOE retired as an Air Force officer before earning an MFA from Bennington College. His chapbook, *Brass*, won the Kinloch Rivers contest in 2006. He served in Vietnam, as J-2 at COMUSFORCARIB during Grenada, and in several assignments for DIA.

HUGH MARTIN is a veteran of the Iraq War and a graduate of Muskingum University. His chapbook, *So, How Was the War?* (Kent State UP, 2010) was published by the Wick Poetry Center, and his first book, *The Stick Soldiers,* won the 2012 A. Poulin Jr. Poetry prize, and will be released through BOA Editions, Ltd. in March, 2013. Recent work of his has appeared in *The Kenyon Review, Crazyhorse,* and *The American Poetry Review.* He recently completed his MFA at Arizona State and will be a Stegner Fellow at Stanford University in the fall of 2012.

FRED MCGAVRAN is a graduate of Kenyon College and Harvard Law School, and served as an officer in the Navy in Vietnam. After practicing law for many years, he was ordained a deacon in The Episcopal Diocese of Southern Ohio, where he serves as Assistant Chaplain at Episcopal Retirement Homes in Cincinnati. He can be found at fredmcgavran.com.

ROBERT MCGOWAN served as a pay disbursement specialist with the Ninth Infantry Division in Vietnam, 1968-69. His fiction and essays are published in over five dozen literary journals in America and abroad and have been four times nominated for the Pushcart Prize. He is the author of the story collections *NAM: Things That Weren't True and Other Stories* and *Stories from the Art World*. He lives in Memphis. His website is robert-mcgowan.com.

WILLIAM MILLER is a poet and children's book author. He has published many poems in literary magazines. He lives in the French Quarter of New Orleans.

MICHAIL W. MULVEY is a retired public-school educator. He served with the 4/23rd Infantry, 25th Infantry Division in Vietnam in 1967. He lives in Connecticut where he is an adjunct lecturer in the English Department at Central Connecticut State University.

ELISABETH MURAWSKI is the author of *Zorba's Daughter*, which won the 2010 May Swenson Poetry Award, *Moon and Mercury*, and two chapbooks. She was a Hawthornden Fellow in 2008. She currently resides in Alexandria, Virginia.

STANLEY NOAH has a BGS degree from the University of Texas at Dallas. He has been published in the *Wisconsin Review, Nexus, South Carolina Review*, and many other publications.

SUSAN O'NEILL is the author of *Don't Mean Nothing* (Ballantine 2001: Serving House Books, 2010), a fiction collection based loosely on her stint as an Army nurse during the Viet Nam war. She edits the flash fiction lit magazine Vestal Review, has published much fiction and non-fiction, and maintains an essay blog ("Off the Matrix") at peacecorpsworldwide.org. She is working on an essay collection entitled *Calling New Delhi for Free.*

JASON POUDRIER has published two collections of poetry: *Red Fields* (Mongrel Empire Press, 2012), and a chapbook, *In the Rubble at Our Feet,* (Rose Rock Press, 2011). His poetry has been anthologized and has appeared in several literary journals. While serving in the Army, he was deployed to Iraq, wounded in action, and awarded the Purple Heart.

LOUIS R. PRINCE is a retired businessman living in Cincinnati, Ohio. He served as an Army Field Artillery Officer in World War II from June, 1941 to February, 1946, primarily in the Ninth Infantry Division. His decorations include the Bronze Star, the Purple Heart, and the French Legion of Honor.

RUSSELL REECE has had stories and essays published in *Memoir (and), Crimespree Magazine, Delaware Beach Life, Sliver of Stone, The Fox Chase Review* and other online and print journals. Russ is a University of Delaware alumnus and a board member of the Delaware Literary Connection. He lives in Bethel, Delaware, along the beautiful Broad Creek, and is currently working on a novel set in that area in the 1930s.

CYNTHIA RIS, former attorney, freelance journalist and photographer, teaches English at the University of Cincinnati and works as a freelance editor. Some of her poetry has appeared in *Poem, Home: An Anthology of Ars Poetica, The Innisfree Poetry Journal,* and *Identity Theory.*

NICHOLAS SAMARAS won The Yale Series of Younger Poets Award with his first book, *Hands of the Saddlemaker.* His next book, *American Psalm, World Psalm,* is forthcoming in the spring of 2014 from Ashland Poetry Press.

DON SCHOFIELD's books include *Approximately Paradise, Kindled*

Terraces: American Poets in Greece, and *The Known: The Selected Poems of Nikos Fokas.* A resident of Greece for many years, he currently lives in Thessaloniki where he is the Dean of Special Programs at Perrotis College, the higher education division of the American Farm School.

TOM SHEEHAN served in Korea, 1951, and lives in Saugus, Massachusetts. His books are *Epic Cures* and *Brief Cases, Short Spans,* from Press 53; *A Collection of Friends* and *From the Quickening,* from Pocol Press. His newest, from Milspeak Books, are *Korean Echoes* (2011), and *The Westering* (2012), which will be followed by at least nine more.

HENRY F. TONN is a semi-retired psychologist who has published fiction, nonfiction, and poetry in such literary journals as the *Gettysburg Review, Connecticut Review, Front Porch Journal,* and *Eclectica.* He lives with his Chow dog, Fred, in Wilmington, North Carolina. His website is henrytonn.com.

LAURENCE W. THOMAS lived in war-torn Europe and the Middle East, then compiled his reactions to man's treatment of his fellow man in a book of poetry, *Man's Wolf to Man.* His experiences at home and abroad have informed his poetry and directed his interests. "Dissolution" is an amalgam of thoughts about the effects of war.

ML

2-13